D1525250

GRAVE MISGIVINGS

A MADDIE GRAVES MYSTERY BOOK FOUR

LILY HARPER HART

HARPERHART PUBLICATIONS

Copyright © 2015 by Lily Harper Hart

All rights reserved.

No part of this book may be reproduced in any form or by any electronic or mechanical means, including information storage and retrieval systems, without written permission from the author, except for the use of brief quotations in a book review.

❀ Created with Vellum

1. ONE

"Marco."

"Polo."

Nick Winters smiled when he heard the melodic sound of his girlfriend's voice. He shifted quickly, his eyes scanning the dark field for a glimpse of honey-colored hair. He exhaled shallowly as he tried to keep his exact position something of a mystery and listened for the telltale snap of a branch that would hint at Maddie's location.

Summer was officially here, and even though northern Lower Michigan wasn't mired in a heat wave, the nights were pleasant enough to enjoy a moonlit picnic. This was Nick's favorite time of year, and the fact that he was spending his summer (finally!) with the love of his life made things even more special.

Now he just had to find her.

After June kicked off with a heat wave, temperatures settled into a more normal pattern. Three months of sun, fun, and love were ahead of him, and Nick didn't want to miss a second of it. That's why he suggested a romantic picnic with his best-friend-turned-girlfriend, Maddie Graves.

Her house was currently undergoing construction, an apartment for her elderly grandmother, Maude, being erected in the spot where the garage used to be. In addition to the apartment, the master suite on the second floor was undergoing a spruce so Nick could move into the house with Maddie in a few weeks. They spent every night together as it was, but they would be officially cohabitating in a month. He couldn't wait.

"Marco," he sang out, tilting his head to the side so he could listen closer.

Maddie didn't immediately reply, which made Nick think his comely girlfriend was closer than she wanted to let on. His picnic turned into some heavy petting, which of course, meant Maddie wanted to torture him. They'd played this game so many times as kids he'd lost count. When she suggested playing it as adults – for clothes – Nick jumped at the chance. Now he just wanted to find her.

"You have to play the game right, Maddie," Nick chided, shifting to his right when he thought he heard something behind him. The woods to the north of Maddie's house were dark, but he knew them well enough not to fear tripping over a branch or getting lost. This was their safe haven. This was where they fell in love – even though they were both too young, and scared, to admit it. This would be where they spent their forever.

He just had to win the game first.

"Marco."

The bushes behind Nick exploded as Maddie stepped out. He was in the middle of a heart attack when she wrapped her arms around his waist from behind and kissed his cheek. "Polo. I win."

Nick couldn't hide his grin as he turned, drawing her lithe frame into his arms and giving her a warm hug. "Are you going to think less of me as a man if I admit you just scared the crap out of me?"

"Nothing will make me think less of you as a man," Maddie murmured, lifting her mouth so she could accept his welcoming kiss.

As emotions go, love is a funny one, Nick internally mused. He'd loved Maddie for as long as he could remember, but ten years apart – and a lot of rage – had not diminished the feelings he tried so hard to bury. The second she walked back into his life he'd known nothing had changed. He knew she was his destiny.

Sure, they had a few obstacles to overcome first. There was that pesky little girlfriend problem he had, and the big secret she was hiding. It turned out Maddie didn't run away from Nick after graduation because she didn't love him. No, Maddie ran because she was psychic and could see ghosts – and she misguidedly thought that would disgust him and make him turn on her.

Their past was littered with mistakes, but Nick was convinced their future was rosy and bright. He had everything he'd ever wanted. He was never going to let her go.

"I think you cheated," Nick said, panting slightly as he pulled away from their needy kiss.

"How did I cheat?" Maddie asked, her sea-blue eyes sparkling under the moonlight. "We both started the game at the same time. It's not my fault you're a poor tracker."

Nick snorted. "I'm the best tracker in the world, love," he said, kissing the tip of her nose. "I let you win."

"So, wait ... first I cheated, and now you let me win? Methinks your ego is taking a beating," she teased, her heart-shaped face splitting with a wide grin. "You lost to a girl. Admit it."

"Fine," Nick said. "I lost to a girl. It's not the first thing I've lost to you."

"I told you I misplaced your Detroit Lions sweatshirt years ago," Maddie said. "I'll buy you a new one. I really don't have it anymore."

"I was talking about my heart, Mad," Nick said, tugging on a strand of her blonde hair.

"Oh," she said, sucking her bottom lip into her mouth. He couldn't see her blushing in the limited light, but he knew her well enough to know that was exactly what she was doing.

"It's a good thing you're smoking hot," Nick said, rubbing his hand up and down her back. "You're slow on the uptake sometimes. I've told you I love you so many times I've lost count – and yet you still seem surprised when I say it. We need to work on that."

"I'm not surprised you love me," Maddie corrected. "Well ... maybe a little. I'm just so in love with you that it warms my heart – and face, apparently – when you say it out loud."

"Then I guess I'm just going to have to keep saying it to you for the rest of our lives," Nick said, grabbing her around the waist and swinging her so her feet left the ground. "I always want your heart warm."

Maddie giggled, and after a few more minutes of canoodling, Nick led her back to the blanket they'd spread out in the adjacent field and settled her between his legs so they could cuddle in comfort.

"I love this time of year," Maddie said, leaning her head back against his chest. "When I was down in the city it was hard to get a good look at the moon. It was always loud ... and bright ... and lonely ... but I feel so happy here with you."

"I always want you to be happy, Mad," Nick said, nuzzling her neck. "This is my favorite time of year, too."

"The Fourth of July is coming up on Monday," Maddie said. "That means we have an extended weekend. I was thinking of closing the shop up tomorrow and Friday and clearing my schedule."

Nick moved his hands up to her neck and mindlessly started massaging it. Now that she'd brought up the holiday weekend, he had a little subject of his own to broach – and he wasn't sure how she would take it.

"Do you not want to spend the weekend with me?" Maddie asked, causing Nick to realize he'd left her hanging. "Do you have to work, or ... do you have other plans?"

She was feeling insecure, and Nick internally cursed himself for letting it happen. She was much more comfortable with their relationship these days, and she had faith he would always be there for her, but he forgot that she still worried from time to time. She couldn't see inside his heart. She couldn't see she was all he thought about ... or wanted. He still had to take the time to tell her.

"Maddie, I want to spend every weekend with you for the rest of our lives," Nick said, pausing from his neck ministrations to lower his mouth and kiss the tender slope that led to her ear. "I'm actually thrilled that you cleared your schedule. I have the whole weekend off, too."

"You do?"

"I put in for it right after we got together," he said. "I thought there were about a hundred different ways we could light off some fireworks – and I didn't want to miss any of them."

Maddie poked his ribs, rolling her eyes as she shifted her face in his direction. "You have a one-track mind."

"And you're the track," Nick said.

"So, what do you want to do? It's too bad Granny's apartment isn't finished yet. We're not going to find a lot of privacy in the big house. We can stay out at your house, though. You don't have a lot of time left to enjoy it before we move in together."

"Well, actually … ."

"What aren't you telling me?" Maddie asked, her brow furrowing. "You're making me nervous."

"There's nothing to be nervous about, love," Nick said. "I just … do you know what else is going on this weekend?"

"There's a fair downtown."

"There's always a fair downtown," Nick said, rolling his eyes. "It's Blackstone Bay. If it's summer and there's not a fair it's only because someone hasn't figured out what to celebrate yet. That's not what I was talking about, though."

Maddie waited.

"It's our high school reunion, Mad," Nick prodded. "Everyone is getting together Monday at the pavilion to hang out."

"Oh," Maddie said, stiffening in his arms. "I forgot all about that."

Nick snuggled her closer, trying to push the negative emotions rolling off of her away. "I know you don't have the best memories of high school, Mad, but things will be different now."

"I have horrible memories of high school," Maddie corrected. "Horrible."

"Love, not all your memories of that time can be bad," Nick said. "We were together then. We had a lot of fun."

"You and I did, yes," Maddie said. "I don't care about any of those other people."

"What about Christy?" Nick asked, referring to Maddie's boisterous friend. "She'll be there."

"I ... I see her all the time," Maddie said. "I don't need to see her when those other people are around."

"Mad," Nick groaned. "It's been ten years. High school is rough on a lot of people. When you grow up things change. I promise things will be better. Don't you want to go to the reunion?"

"No."

Nick cocked his head to the side, trying to determine the best way to approach the situation. Maddie had a right to her feelings, and her high school existence had been plagued by horrors of the teenage girl persuasion. Mean girls exist in every time and every school, and Maddie was a regular target for a specific group of girls. Still ... . "Mad, Marla Proctor was the one who tortured you in high school," he said. "You've already seen her – numerous times, mind you – since you've been back."

"I ... ."

"Shh," Nick admonished her. "Marla is a horrible person. She wants to make others unhappy because she's unhappy. You can't change that. She's the exception, not the rule."

"You want to go," Maddie said, worrying her bottom lip with her teeth.

"I do."

"I ... you can go without me."

"I'm not doing that," Nick said, his voice firm. "If you don't want to go then I'm not going to go."

"Oh, that's not fair," Maddie protested. "You're putting this all on me. Now I'm going to be the reason you don't go. That's just so ... mean."

"I know," Nick said. "It's the way of the world, though, Mad. You're my girlfriend. I've finally managed to snag you. I want to show you off in front of the guys, and I want you on my arm when they see you in a nice dress and are green with envy because I'm clearly the one who ended up with the happiest life."

"Oh, good grief," Maddie grumbled.

"Come on, Mad," Nick prodded. "I promise, if you're uncomfortable, I'll take you home. I won't make you stay. You know I'll be right there with you."

"Fine." Maddie gave in. His pleading face was too much for her to deny. "You can't leave me alone, though."

"I never want to leave you alone, love." He kissed her softly.

"Are you happy?"

"Almost," Nick said. "That was just the first thing I wanted to talk to you about."

"Oh, this is going to be bad," Maddie said, crossing her arms over her chest. "You just suckered me in and now you're going to drop the hammer on me."

"What hammer?"

Maddie narrowed her eyes.

Nick sighed, tamping down his frustration. "Do you remember Aaron Denton?"

"The rich kid who lived in the Denton mansion on the north side of town? Yeah, I remember him. I always wanted to see his house. I heard it has a cemetery and mausoleum on the grounds, and the river supposedly runs right up to the back patio."

"It does. It's a cool place."

Maddie made a face. "I was never invited to his house because I was unpopular."

"You were invited to his house because he wanted to hit on you," Nick countered. "Don't even pretend otherwise. You just refused to go because you were so unsure of yourself back then. I was there. Don't bother lying to me."

"Whatever."

Nick rested his chin on her shoulder. "The good news is that you have a chance to see the house now," he said.

"I do?"

"We've been invited to spend the weekend out there," Nick said. "It's going to be like a big party. There's going to be a handful of people from our graduating class staying there. They've even got a bunch of maids and cooks ... so it will be like staying in a hotel."

"I don't know ... ."

"Mad, it will be good for you," Nick said. "It will give us a chance to get away from Maude for the weekend. The river is right there so we can get some fishing and kayaking in. There will be other people there to hang out with if we want ... and if we want to be alone, the house is set on a hundred acres of property. We won't have to see people if we don't feel like it."

"You really want to go, don't you?"

"I wouldn't mind hanging out with some of the guys from high school," Nick said, choosing his words carefully. "I want to be with you regardless, though. Going to the reunion is enough. If this is too much for you ... ."

"We'll go."

Her decisiveness surprised Nick. "We will?"

"You've been going out of your way to make sure I get everything I want since we got together," Maddie said. "I think it's my turn to give you what you want. I do reserve the right to leave if things get too ... weird, though."

"Why would they get weird?"

"I'm psychic and I can see ghosts, Nicky," Maddie said. "Things always get weird around me."

"I guess it's good that I like weird things then," Nick teased, kissing her cheek. "I know I've told you this before, but being psychic doesn't define you. It's something you can do ... and I'm proud of everything about you."

"Thank you."

"I love you, Maddie," Nick said. "I love you with everything that I am. If you get uncomfortable, we'll go. I just ... thank you for giving this a chance."

"I would do anything for you, Nicky," Maddie said. "You're my whole heart."

"Good," Nick said. "I'm glad we both feel the same way. Now ... about our game ... I believe I owe you some nudity since you won."

Maddie smiled despite herself. "I want a little dance, too."

"You know I don't have any rhythm."

"That's why it's funny."

"Love, just a tip, but men don't like women who laugh when they're naked," Nick said.

"I'll take that under advisement," Maddie said. "Now ... get stripping."

"Yes, love."

2. TWO

"What's up, girlfriend?"

Christy Ford was a bundle of energy on a normal day, but if Maddie was any judge of her friend's moods, she was especially excited today. Her bouncy red hair was brighter than normal, and her smile was so wide it overshadowed the rest of her cute face as she bustled around her hair salon, Cuts & Curls.

"What's up with you?" Maddie asked, lifting an eyebrow.

"I'm just in a good mood," Christy said. "I love this time of year. It's second only to Christmas for me. In fact, it's like Christmas in July."

Maddie smiled, Christy's good mood was too infectious to ignore. "I love summer, too. Although, if I'm being honest, Halloween is my favorite time of year."

Christy wrinkled her pert nose. "Why?"

"I just like multicolored leaves and horror movies," Maddie said.

"You're weird."

"I can't explain it."

"Not that I'm not happy to see you, but what are you doing here?" Christy asked, handing one of her workers a bottle of conditioner before moving over to her own station at the front of the salon.

"I was hoping you could cut a couple inches off my hair," Maddie admitted, instinctively running her fingers through her long, blonde locks. It was her trademark, and she didn't want to cut it too short, but she wanted to ease up on the length just a bit.

"You never want to cut your hair," Christy said.

"You've cut my hair four times since I got back to town," Maddie protested.

"I've trimmed your hair four times since you came back," Christy countered. "Basically I've cut the very tips of your hair off. That's all you've trusted me to do."

"I ... I trust you," Maddie said, here eyes widening. "It's just ... my hair is one of my favorite things."

"Your hair is beautiful," Christy said, reaching over so she could grab a strand of Maddie's hair to study it. "People would pay thousands of dollars to get this color. It's long without being straggly. Your face is heart-shaped, so your hair offsets it nicely. Your hair is breathtaking."

"So you think I shouldn't cut it?" Maddie was starting to worry.

"How many inches are we talking here?" Christy asked.

"Two."

Christy snorted. "I think that's a healthy haircut," she said. "I also think you and Nick are the only ones who are going to notice it. Your hair is really long."

"Maybe I shouldn't," Maddie hedged, biting her lower lip. "Nick loves my hair long."

"Sit down," Christy ordered, rolling her eyes. "I promise you'll be happy when I'm done."

Maddie climbed onto the chair and leaned forward so Christy could drape a protective smock over her. "Don't go crazy."

"I never go crazy," Christy said, grabbing a bottle of water from the counter and spraying Maddie's hair. "So, tell me, how is the construction going?"

"It's not too bad," Maddie said. "I kind of wish I would've had them finish the upstairs bedroom before starting on Granny's apartment, but it's too late now."

"Why?"

"They're refinishing the hardwood floors and there's dust every-where," Maddie said. "I had to hang some of those plastic sheets at the top of the staircase so the dust doesn't drift down into the store, but people are traipsing in and out ... and Granny refuses to wear the little plastic booties when she's up there ... so it's still a mess."

Christy smirked. "It won't take long," she said. "Just think, when it's all finished, you're going to move into the big room with Nick. That has to be exciting."

"It is," Maddie conceded. "I'm a little nervous, though."

"Why?"

"I ... he's going to see me all the time, even when I'm at my worst."

Christy waited for Maddie to expand.

"My hair is a mess in the morning."

"You guys haven't spent a night apart since you got together," Christy pointed out. "He's already seen you at your worst. I should point out, though, that your worst isn't bad so you should probably shut up if you don't want people to hate you."

Maddie made a face. "I ... I'm sorry."

"You should be."

"I can't decide if you're good for my ego or bad for my self-esteem," Maddie said.

"I'm both," Christy replied, nonplussed. "You're a beautiful woman, Maddie Graves. Sometimes I think you purposely don't see it because you think it makes you vain. Other times I think you're fishing for compliments."

"I am not!"

Christy grinned. "It's okay to fish for compliments," she said. "Everyone does it. I just wish you'd admit you're doing it."

"I hate you sometimes," Maddie grumbled, crossing her arms over her chest.

"Well, I love you," Christy said. "What are you and Nick doing this weekend? Are you looking forward to the reunion?"

"I wasn't going to go until Nick sprung it on me last night," Maddie replied. "I honestly forgot all about it."

"Why weren't you going to go?"

"No offense to you, but I hate everyone we went to high school with."

"No offense taken, *bitch*," Christy deadpanned.

Maddie rolled her eyes. "It's just ... high school was a really hard time for me," she said. "I was always so nervous ... and uncomfortable in my own skin. I had a hard time fitting in, and it always felt as if people were staring at me."

"You went through an awkward phase in middle school, like everyone does," Christy said. "Somewhere after sophomore year, though, you blossomed. I remember when everyone came back from summer break before junior year started. All the guys were buzzing about the 'new' girl in school.

"The thing is, there wasn't a new girl," she continued. "It was you. I remember you sprouted like two inches in three months, and your boobs filled out, and every guy in school decided you were the one they wanted to get."

"That didn't happen," Maddie said.

"Yes, it did," Christy said. "You were in your own little world, so you probably didn't realize it, but it definitely happened. The entire football team had a bet to see who was going to get the first date with you."

Maddie stilled. "Nick was on the football team."

"He was the only one who didn't play the game," Christy said hurriedly, not wanting to cause problems between Maddie and her heart's desire. "Trust me. He was nothing but respectful where you were concerned.

"The problem for poor Nick was that he'd gone through the whole summer with you and somehow managed not to notice all the changes your body was going through," she said. "I think it was just one of those mind-over-matter things. He didn't want to see it, so he didn't see it. The more the football team talked, though, the more Nick realized you were hot."

"It's a little weird that you know all of this," Maddie said.

"I was in the band," Christy said. "Talk about geeky ... ugh." She shuddered and then returned to the moment. "I heard all the gossip because we practiced on the field next to the football team. You were the topic of conversation for weeks."

"What did Nick do?" Maddie was interested, despite herself.

"Well, at first he pretended he didn't notice what everyone was saying," Christy said. "He tried to ignore it when everyone talked about your legs ... and boobs ... and butt."

"You're making me uncomfortable," Maddie warned.

Christy winked into the mirror. "I do remember one specific blowup," she said. "Brian Franz told everyone he was going to sneak over to your house and spy on you because he was desperate to see you naked. Nick completely freaked out and beat the crap out of him. Brian had a black eye for two weeks."

Maddie frowned. "I ... that's why Brian and Nick fought? Nick said it was an accident on the football field that got out of hand."

"I think it definitely got out of hand, but it wasn't an accident," Christy said. "I know that Brian was begging Nick to get off of him by the end and he promised he would never even do so much as look at you again as long as Nick stopped hitting him. That's when everyone knew."

"Knew what?"

"That you and Nick were destined," Christy said. "Everyone knew you guys were close up until that point. No one – especially you two, apparently – knew that you were in love."

"I don't know what to say to that," Maddie admitted. "I ... part of me is happy to hear it. Does that make me a horrible person?"

"It makes you human," Christy said. "I'm glad, too. I was a little worried you were an alien because you were so perfect."

"Okay, you're officially good for my ego," Maddie conceded. "I'm a little worried about something else, though."

"What?"

"Aaron Denton invited Nick to stay at his house this weekend as part of the reunion celebration," Maddie said. "I agreed to go with him, and I'm really nervous. I never hung around with that crowd in high school. Nick did sometimes, but I only hung around with Nick when it was just the two of us."

"Oh, you're going to Aaron's?" Christy looked surprised. "I am, too."

"You are?" Maddie didn't realize she was holding her breath until it whooshed out. "I've never been happier to hear anything in my entire life."

"Six weeks ago Nick Winters admitted you were the love of his life and he wanted to spend forever with you," Christy said. "You're saying the fact that I'm going to be staying at the Denton mansion with you this weekend is better news than that?"

Maddie's smile was rueful. "You have a way of putting things into perspective."

"I do," Christy said. "It's going to be okay, Maddie. "I don't think there are going to be a lot of people there. I heard it's only going to be like eight or nine of us total. That's not a lot of people. It will be good for you."

"You sound like Nick," Maddie muttered.

"Nick loves you more than anything else in this world," Christy said. "He would never let anything bad happen to you. This weekend is going to be a way for you to put a lot of those high school insecurities behind you.

"Think about it. You grew up to own your own magic store and you're practically engaged to your dream man," she said. "You're on top of the world. Do you really think people you didn't take the time to know in high school are going to tear you down?"

"I guess not," Maddie said. "I ... they didn't take the time to get to know me either."

"It wasn't for lack of trying," Christy said. "I'll admit that a lot of the girls didn't want to get to know you because they were jealous, but almost all of the boys – even most of the gay ones – wanted to know you. You were just ... standoffish."

Maddie made a face. "I wasn't standoffish."

"Fine," Christy said, holding her hands up in mock surrender. "I shouldn't have used that word. That makes you sound like a snob, and you're definitely not a snob. You were isolated, though.

"Listen, I know why you were like that now," she said. "You were scared to death people were going to find out ... certain things ... about you. Personally, I think that would've made you even more popular, but what do I know? It's different now. You're an adult. It's going to be fun. I promise."

"I hate to say it, but I feel so much better knowing you're going to be there, too," Maddie said. "I was worried I was going to cling to Nick and smother him because I was afraid to interact with everyone else."

"I think Nick likes to be smothered. I wouldn't worry about that."

"You know what I mean."

"I do," Christy said. "I'm really looking forward to this weekend. We're going to have a good time. We're going to get drunk ... and we're going to gossip ... and I'm hoping some of the guys have aged well enough for me to get lucky and still retain my dignity the next morning."

"You are so gross," Maddie said, chuckling.

"I am," Christy said. "I'm also done with your cut." She twirled Maddie around so she could look at the back of her hair. "What do you think?"

"It looks good," Maddie said. "I ... feel good."

"You should feel good," Christy said. "Your life is practically perfect right now. You don't have anything to complain about."

"I don't," Maddie said. "Are you going to the bonfire tonight?"

"I would never miss the traditional Fourth of July celebratory bonfire," Christy said. "I look great in the romantic light given off by a huge bonfire. Men are going to be falling at my feet. Why do you think I brightened up my hair?"

"You really are ... something," Maddie said.

"I try," Christy said. "I'll see you at the bonfire tonight, and if I don't, I'll definitely see you at Aaron's house tomorrow night."

"I'm actually excited to see the house," Maddie said. "I've heard it's spectacular."

"You pick weird things to be excited about," Christy said. "Here I am excited to get hammered and lucky, and you're excited because you want to see the mansion."

"I want to see the mausoleum, too," Maddie said.

"Weirdo!"

3. THREE

"Why are you packing?"

Olivia Graves popped into view, her gaze immediately falling on the open suitcase on Maddie's bed. Even though her mother died months before, Olivia's soul remained behind, popping in from time to time to visit. Maddie was glad to have her any way she could get her, but she missed being able to hug her.

"I'm going out to Aaron Denton's house for a reunion party this weekend," Maddie said, smiling at her mother. "By the way ... we need to work out a system for you to pop in once Nick and I move to your bedroom. Things might get ... awkward ... otherwise."

Olivia smirked. "Don't worry. I always listen before I leap. I won't embarrass you. In fact, I think it might be wise to have a 'no bedroom' rule from here on out."

"Oh, I don't know if that's necessary," Maddie said.

"Well, how about we make a rule that I can't pop in unless I'm sure you and Nick aren't doing anything," Olivia suggested.

Maddie's cheeks flushed with color, and she averted her eyes from her mother's ghostly orbs. "Mom."

"You're so cute sometimes, Sunshine." Olivia's ghostly hand brushed against Maddie's cheek, and her daughter believed she could almost feel the touch. She definitely felt the love behind the gesture.

"Thanks, Mom," Maddie said dryly.

"So ... why are you going to Aaron Denton's house?"

"He invited us, and Nick really wants to go," Maddie said.

"Don't you want to go?"

"Not really."

"Maddie, you can't go through life being scared of your own shadow," Olivia said. "You're not the same girl you were when you left after high school. You've grown as a person, and you're a strong woman. This is going to be good for you."

"Why does everyone keep telling me that?"

"Who is everyone?"

"Christy and Nick."

"Maybe because those are the two people who know you best ... other than your grandmother and me, that is. Speaking of, where is Mom?"

"I'll get her," Maddie said, sticking her head out the bedroom door. "Granny? Mom is here if you want me to share messages before I go to the bonfire tonight."

"Oh, it's the Fourth of July bonfire," Olivia said. "I always loved a good bonfire."

"I know," Maddie said. "That was one of the town celebrations you refused to miss every year."

"Is Nick picking you up?"

"Yeah. I decided to get a head start on the packing for tomorrow because I figured we would be out at the bonfire late tonight. The problem is, I have no idea what to pack for a weekend at someone's fancy mansion."

At that moment Maddie's grandmother, Maude, shuffled into the room with a wide smile on her face. She must have heard the tail end of Maddie's statement because she instantly started searching through Maddie's dresser. "Tell your mother I said hi."

"Granny, she can hear you," Maddie said. "You can talk to her like you normally would and I'll just repeat what she says back to you."

"Don't get fresh, missy," Maude said. "I know how it works."

The magical peculiarity that flowed through the Graves genes skipped Maude, and while the elderly woman had always been happy about that development, now that her lack of supernatural powers kept her from talking to her only daughter, she was mildly bitter. Maddie internally chastised herself for forgetting how desperately her grandmother wanted to hear Olivia's voice. "I'm sorry, Granny."

"How many times do I have to tell you that I don't like it when you call me that?"

"Just a few hundred more, Granny," Maddie teased, smiling at her persnickety grandmother.

"How long are you going to be staying at Aaron Denton's house?" Maude asked.

"A few nights ... three, I think. Are you okay with that, or do you want me to stay home with you?"

Maude made a face. "Oh, please, you are not using me as an excuse not to go," she said. "I'm perfectly happy to stay home alone. It will give me a chance to walk around the house naked."

Now it was Maddie's turn to make a face. "Excuse me?"

"I like to free my bits from time to time," Maude said. "I'll be able to do it as much as I want when my apartment is finished, but since you came home, I've had to be careful because you're such a prude."

"I am not a prude," Maddie protested. She turned to her mother for support. "Tell her I'm not a prude."

"Of course you're not a prude," Olivia said.

"She said ... ."

"She coddles you," Maude said. "That's why she said it. You're definitely a prude."

Maddie rolled her eyes. "Do you want to help me pack for the weekend, or are you going to ... be you?"

"I'm going to help you pack," Maude said, her eyes sparkling. "I think you're going to need my help so you don't pack a whole suitcase of Amish clothing."

"I don't have Amish clothing."

"You could've fooled me," Maude said, turning her attention to Maddie's closet. "Do you know what you're going to be doing while you're out there? I hear they have a river that runs right up to the back deck, by the way. That sounds really cool."

"It does," Maddie agreed. "As for what we're doing, though, I honestly don't have a clue. I'm guessing I should take a mixture of stuff."

"I'm betting there will be a few dinner parties," Maude said, shifting toward the closet. "You have that nice black dress Christy loaned you, but I don't think you own anything else that's not Amish."

Maddie growled, causing Olivia to giggle.

"I miss you, Mom," Olivia whispered.

Maddie glanced at her, her expression sober.

"Don't tell her I said that until you're leaving," Olivia said, never moving her eyes from Maude. "I want that to be the last thing she hears before I leave tonight."

Maddie nodded silently. "Granny, what about that blue dress?"

Maude pulled the dress in question out of the closet and immediately started shaking her head. "Absolutely not."

"Oh, good, I'm not too late," Christy said, breezing into the room with a garment bag in her arms.

"Oh, it's Christy," Olivia said, her face brightening. "I love her hair. She always has such good energy. Did I tell you how happy I am that you two became friends?"

"I'm happy, too," Maddie said.

"What are you happy about?" Christy asked.

"Oh," Maddie said. "I was just ... ." She broke off, unsure how to answer.

"Olivia is here," Maude said, not missing a beat. "She was probably saying something to her. What's in that bag?"

"Well, I got to thinking after Maddie left the salon today," Christy said. "I knew she probably didn't have many dresses to choose from that didn't make her look like she should be churning butter on a farm with no electricity."

"I told you that you looked Amish sometimes," Maude said, lifting an eyebrow.

"Thank you both so much," Maddie grumbled.

"I have some dresses for you," Christy said. "Oh, and hello, Olivia. I really do miss you."

"I can't borrow more of your dresses," Maddie protested.

"You're not borrowing them," Christy said. "I'm giving them to you."

"What? No."

"It's fine," Christy said. "I have a dress problem. For years, I kept buying these tiny little dresses that I knew I would never be thin enough to fit into – and yet I kept buying them. In the back of my mind, I think I honestly thought my boobs and butt would miraculously shrink."

Christy unzipped the bag.

"Now, I'm a good four inches shorter than you, but I have three dresses here that I think are going to be long enough on you," she said. She pulled the first out, a spaghetti strap floral dress that boasted simple lines and bohemian tassels along the skirt. She held it up against Maddie's body and smiled. "Perfect."

The dress fell to the middle of Maddie's thigh, causing her immediately to start shaking her head. "It's too short."

"It's a perfect length, dear," Olivia said. "The tassels make the dress look longer than it is. The pinks, blues, and purples are going to make your eyes pop, too. It's beautiful."

"Mom, I can't wear this dress," Maddie said. "I'll feel … naked. What would I even wear underneath it?"

"See, I knew that was going to be your first response," Christy said, wagging her finger. She shuffled over to Maddie's dresser and opened the third drawer, rummaging around until she returned with a glittery blue tank top. "You can wear this underneath it. The colors match perfectly, and it will allow you to keep your modesty intact."

Once Christy paired the tank top with the dress, Maddie saw the ensemble's potential. She wasn't quite ready to give in, though. "I don't know … I think that's going to make me look slutty."

"You have no idea what slutty really is," Christy said. "This dress is actually quite modest. It's simple enough that you'll feel comfortable, and dressy enough for a dinner at the Denton house."

"But ... ."

"Nick wants to parade you around, Maddie," Christy said, pulling out the big guns. "Don't you want him to have something to be proud of?"

"Oh, that was well played," Olivia said, silently applauding.

"Don't encourage her," Maddie grumbled.

"Your mother agrees with me, doesn't she?" Christy asked.

"Of course she agrees," Maude said. "I do, too. What other dresses are in there?"

Maddie only kept half an ear on the rest of the conversation. She was resigned to packing whatever else Christy had in the garment bag. She didn't even put up a fight when Christy and Maude started picking lingerie out. By the time they were done, the entire suitcase was packed – including shoes.

"I think that's everything," Christy said, dusting her hands off. "You're going to be the belle of the mansion."

"You're so funny," Maddie deadpanned.

"I try.:

"What's going on up here?" Nick asked, stepping into the room and glancing around. "Is this a ... girl thing? Should I wait in the hallway?"

"We were helping her pack for the weekend," Christy said. "I brought some dresses over that I think you're going to love."

Nick flashed Christy a grateful smile. "Thanks. I always like it when you pick out her clothes. You know how to show her assets off in the best possible way."

"I am gifted," Christy agreed.

"My mother is here," Maddie hissed. "You can't say stuff like that in front of her."

"I take it back," Olivia said. "You are a prude."

"I'm not a prude."

Nick smirked. "I happen to love my prude," he said. "Did you make sure to pack regular clothes, too? I figured we would be spending half our day in the river."

"I packed a bathing suit, shorts, and my J-41 recreation shoes," Maddie said. "That should be good, right?"

"That's should be fine," Nick said. "The good thing is that we're going to be close enough to home to pop over to get something if we need it."

"Call before you pop," Maude warned. "I have plans."

Nick narrowed his eyes. "What plans? You're not planning on doing something to Harriet, are you? If you get arrested, I'm leaving you in jail until the holiday weekend is over."

"My love for you goes as fast as it comes," Maude said.

Nick grinned. "Seriously, what are your plans?"

"Don't worry about it," Maude said. "I'm not doing anything scandalous."

"You told me you were going to air your bits out and walk around the house naked the whole weekend," Maddie said.

Nick's face colored at the visual while Christy burst into hysterical gales of laughter.

"You have a really big mouth sometimes," Maude chided, wagging her finger in Maddie's face.

"I'm sorry, Granny," Maddie said. "You did say that, though."

Maude wrinkled her nose, and Maddie could practically see her mind working. She had a feeling Maude was thinking of something to say that would embarrass Maddie ... and she was right.

"Don't worry, Nick. I'm the one who picked Maddie's lingerie for the weekend. Every time she puts it on, I want you to think of me picking it out for her."

Nick swallowed hard. "I ... ."

"Oh, that's so cute," Olivia cooed.

"I just want to bottle the look on Nick's face and sell it," Christy said. "It's priceless. I'd be a rich woman if I could manage that."

"Okay," Nick said, clearing his throat. "On that note, I think we're done here. Maddie, my love, are you ready for our first bonfire night as a couple?"

Maddie smiled. "I'm ready for everything we do as a couple."

Nick's face softened and he extended his hand. "Come on, then. I figured we could walk. Since I'm off duty, I thought a few drinks would benefit both of us. If you're a very good girl, I might even dance with you."

"We're trying to make her less of a prude," Maude said. "We don't want her to be a good girl."

"Okay, I think I've had just about enough of you for one night," Nick said. "Behave yourself."

"I'm old," Maude said. "You get to misbehave when you're old. It's the only good thing about aging."

"Fine," Nick said. "Be as bad as you want to be. Just ... make sure you're clothed by the time we get back."

"Make sure you call before you come back," Maude countered.

Nick pinched the bridge of his nose to ward off the oncoming headache. "You make me tired."

"Welcome to my world," Maddie said.

Nick linked his fingers with Maddie's and started tugging her out of the room. "Your grandmother is not allowed in our bedroom once we move," he said. "I'm going to have nightmares about her and your lingerie. You know that, right?"

"Oh, wait ... ." Maddie pulled away from him long enough to stick her head back in the bedroom. "Mom says she misses you very much, Granny."

Maude beamed at Maddie, a lone tear trailing down her cheek. "You're a good girl, Maddie Graves."

"Thank you, Granny."

"You're still a prude."

"Thank you, Granny."

4. FOUR

"Wow. It's so ... busy," Maddie said, gripping Nick's hand tightly as she looked around Blackstone Bay's bustling town square. "A lot of people must have come back to town for the reunion."

"Does that make you nervous?"

"It makes me glad that I have you," Maddie replied, glancing at him for reassurance.

"You're going to have me for the rest of your life and beyond, my Maddie," Nick said, leaning over and giving her a soft kiss. "I love you. If you get uncomfortable ... ."

"No. I need to stop being such a ... ."

"Prude?"

Maddie scowled. "I was going to say mouse."

"You're not a mouse, Mad," Nick said, pulling her in front of him so he could wrap his arms around her waist. "You're just the type of woman who likes to think things over before you act. That's not necessarily a bad thing."

"You make me sound boring."

"Oh, don't even go there," Nick said, nuzzling her cheek. "You're the most interesting person I know."

"I think you're just saying that because you want sex later."

Nick grinned. "I want you, Mad. Sex is merely a bonus."

"You're such smooth talker."

"That's why you love me, right?" Nick lowered his mouth and kissed her again, sinking into the exchange.

They were so lost in each other they didn't notice two shadows heading in their direction. By the time the dark figures were on Nick and Maddie, it was too late.

"Wow, Winters, are you going to give her your tongue to keep?"

Nick pulled away from Maddie reluctantly, rolling his eyes until they landed on the two men watching them. "Aaron. Brian. How are you guys?"

"Not as good as you apparently."

Nick extended his hand to greet his old friends, but before he got the chance the two men engulfed him in bear hugs. There were numerous laughs, and a few veiled insults, but everything was in jest.

Maddie watched, shifting uncomfortably as Nick seamlessly interacted with Aaron and Brian. It gave her a chance to look them over. High school was ten years behind them, but very little had changed about either man. They were both broad and tall, wide shoulders giving way to strong chests and tapering down to narrow waists. Their hair was shorter, and their eyes were keen and interested as they chatted with Nick.

Finally, Aaron shifted his attention from Nick and focused on Maddie. "Well, Maddie Graves, you grew up to be ... ."

"Be careful," Nick warned.

"A very attractive woman," Aaron said.

Nick slipped his arm around Maddie's waist and tugged her to his side. "She is a very attractive woman," he agreed. "*My* attractive woman."

"Oh, good grief," Brian said. "Are we going to go through this again? Everyone knows Maddie is with you, Nick. In fact, the second she returned to town my mother called to see if I wanted a spot in the pool for when you two would get together. I was way off. I thought you two would be on each other that first week."

Maddie made a face while Nick grinned. "I should've moved faster. I know."

Maddie poked him in the ribs. "Don't encourage them," she said. "You know I don't like all the pools."

"I heard Maude won the sex pool," Aaron said, ignoring Maddie's discomfort. "Personally, I think she should be exempt from the pools because she has inside information, but I don't get a say in it."

Maddie was mortified, and when Nick glanced down at her he could read the expression on her face. "Are you okay?"

"It's fine," Maddie said, waving off his concerns and inhaling a steadying breath. "I'm used to it now. Everyone in town knows exactly when we do everything. I'm considering putting my own money in the next pool."

Nick smirked. "Really?"

"Hey, if you can't beat them … ."

"So, Maddie, I have to admit something to you," Brian said. "I had a huge crush on you back in high school. I was dying to ask you out. When I mentioned my intentions, though, Nick lost his cool and beat me up. Even back then he was crazy about you."

Nick's cheeks burned, and he was scared to meet Maddie's steady gaze. He'd never told her the real reason he'd fought with Brian, instead making up an excuse to explain the bruise on his cheek.

"I heard about that," Maddie said, placing her tongue in her cheek to keep from laughing. "The thing is, I heard you were planning on coming over to my house so you could spy through the window and see me naked. I didn't hear anything about you asking me out on a date."

Nick stilled as Brian uncomfortably coughed.

"I … um … ." Brian stammered and stared at his feet.

"Who told you that?" Nick asked.

"A little birdie," Maddie replied, enjoying her moment of power.

"I told her," Christy said, sidling up to the group. "Hey, guys."

"Christy!" Aaron grabbed the boisterous redhead and exuberantly swung her around. "You look hot!"

"I know," Christy said, smoothing her shirt down after returning to the ground. "I'll bet you wish you'd looked beyond my geeky band hat and dated me when we were in high school now, don't you?"

"You have no idea," Aaron said, shooting her a flirty wink.

Brian greeted Christy with a more muted hug and a scowl. "Why did you tell Maddie that?"

"Because I wanted to see her face when she heard the truth," Christy said, refusing to back down. "It was priceless."

"You know, I'm usually all for Maddie hanging out with you," Nick said. "I'm starting to rethink it, though."

"You'll get over it when you see the dresses I packed for her," Christy shot back. "Get over yourself. I thought she deserved to know that you were fighting for her honor back then. The story makes you look like a hero. I don't know why you're whining like a baby."

"I'm not whining."

"When I look at you the only thing I see missing is the diaper," Christy said. "Besides, it's not like I told her about the time you threatened to run Max Joseph over because he was making noises about trying to take her up to Kissing Point."

Nick pressed his lips together, horrified.

Maddie took pity on him and squeezed his hand. "I'm flattered."

"I know you're just saying that to make me feel better," Nick said. "I'm going to take it, though."

"Oh, you guys are so cute," Aaron said. "It's like watching a really adorable sitcom couple try to navigate the harsh waters of life."

"I see you're still talking like a woman," Nick said.

"Hey," Maddie and Christy said in unison.

"I happen to love women," Nick said quickly. "This one especial-ly." He dropped a kiss on the top of Maddie's head. "Are you guys done trying to embarrass me?"

"For now," Aaron said. "I think we should get some beers and find a table. Max is supposed to be here, and I heard Lauren is back in town, too."

"Lauren Bishop?" Christy asked, arching an interested eyebrow. "I haven't seen her since graduation."

"Me either," Aaron said. "I'm hoping she's still hot."

"You don't have a chance with her," Brian said.

"You don't know that," Aaron said.

"I do," Brian replied, puffing out his chest. "She's going to want me. We all know I'm the handsome one here. You look old, and you're starting to lose your hair."

Aaron shot him the finger. "I'm going to slip Nair in your conditioner this weekend if you're not careful."

Maddie smiled, enjoying the bragging men and easy repartee even though she didn't feel she knew Brian and Aaron well enough to participate yet. It seemed Nick – and everyone else, for that matter – had been right. The only one standing in Maddie's way was Maddie herself.

"SO, who is going to be staying at your house this weekend?" Nick asked two hours later, swigging from his beer and rubbing Maddie's knee under the picnic table.

Aaron shrugged. "The five of us for sure. Max is going to be there, too, although I have no idea where he is right now. Shouldn't he be here?"

"He's here," Christy said, pointing at the dance floor. "He's already got his eye on something ... slutty, though."

Everyone shifted their eyes in the direction Christy was gesturing, taking in the handsome man, his long black hair brushing the top of his shoulders as he danced with a willowy brunette.

"Who is that?" Aaron asked, narrowing his eyes.

Maddie recognized the familiar silhouette without having to see the woman's face. "Marla Proctor."

Aaron made an exaggerated face. "Oh, I forgot about Marla. How is she?"

"Exactly the same," Nick said, squeezing Maddie's knee reassuringly. "She's still evil."

"She was always evil," Brian said.

"You still slept with her," Christy reminded him.

"Hey, there were only so many girls in high school who would actually put out," Brian said. "She was one of the few. There were plenty of girls who said they put out, but Marla was one of the rare ones who actually did it."

"As far as I can tell, she put out to the entire senior class," Maddie said.

Aaron snorted. "Nice snark, Graves. I didn't think you had it in you."

Maddie blushed. "I ... ."

"Her sarcastic tongue comes and goes," Nick said, grinning as he touched the side of his head to Maddie's. "Besides, Marla didn't put out to everyone in our class. I never slept with her."

"That's because you were mooning over Maddie," Brian teased. "You two spent every waking hour together ... yet there was no tongue action. We were all waiting and waiting ... ."

"Shut up," Nick said. "We were just friends back then."

"Are you really going to sit there and tell me you weren't in love with Maddie back then?" Aaron asked. "Really?"

Nick shrugged. "I've loved her my whole life. I'm not ashamed to admit it."

"But you wouldn't admit it back then," Aaron pressed. "Why not?"

Nick ran his tongue over his teeth, considering how to answer the question. He'd been prepared for this – or, at least he thought he was. He knew everyone would be asking nonstop questions about his relationship with Maddie. He just wasn't sure how much he wanted to volunteer.

"We weren't ready to be together back then," Maddie said, taking Nick by surprise with her fortitude. "We were too young. You guys might think it's funny, but things worked out. We're together now. Isn't that what's important?"

Nick was impressed with her answer.

"It is what's important," Aaron conceded. "I'm still dying to know how you two finally hooked up."

"That's none of your business," Nick said. "I don't kiss and tell."

"They spent a month tiptoeing around each other and then Nick professed his love because he couldn't take another second of being without her," Christy said.

Nick glared at her. "Seriously?"

"It's not like it's a dirty story," Christy said. "You two are moving in together, for crying out loud. Suck it up."

"You suck it up," Nick shot back.

"You ... ."

"Both of you suck it up," Maddie said, cutting off Christy's hot retort. "Everyone is happy. Everyone is having a good time. Do you two need to squabble?"

"No," Nick said, kissing her cheek. "We don't need to squabble, love. In fact, I thought you might want to dance with me before we get going."

"You're leaving already?" Brian asked, disappointed.

"We both have to work tomorrow," Nick said. "Besides, we'll all see each other tomorrow night. I want to dance with my girl and then get some sleep."

"Sleep?" Aaron arched an eyebrow.

"You're a pig," Christy said, punching him lightly on the shoulder. "Leave them alone. They're practically Amish when it comes to the sex talk."

"Why does everyone keep saying I'm Amish?" Maddie asked.

"It's because you're so naturally pretty, love," Nick said, grabbing her hand. "Come dance with me. We'll see you guys tomorrow."

"I'm looking forward to it," Maddie said, surprised to find she actually meant it. "I've always wanted to see your house."

"You could've seen it in high school if Nick wasn't such a protective guard dog where you were concerned." Aaron sent her a saucy wink, which Maddie realized was meant purely as a means to irritate Nick.

"Something tells me that I would've really enjoyed that thirty seconds, but I'm happy to be able to see it now without that hanging over my head," Maddie teased, causing Nick to snicker.

"And that's why she's my girl," he said, slipping his arm around her waist. "We'll see you guys tomorrow."

"Have a good night," Christy said, smiling as they moved away from the table.

Nick kept Maddie close as he led her out to the dance floor, wrapping his arms around her waist and sighing as she lifted her arms to his neck and rested her face against his shoulder.

"Was that too rough for you?" Nick asked after a moment.

"It was fine," Maddie said. "Actually, it was fun. I'm starting to realize that you're right. I do spend too much time in my own head."

"I think your head is a pretty terrific place to be," Nick said, brushing his lips against her forehead. "It's my favorite place in the world."

"I thought my bed was your favorite place in the world."

"It's one of them," Nick said. "Along with our window seat, and your heart."

"Oh, you're so sweet," Maddie said. "Still, I'm tired of being scared of things. I spent years being scared to live my life. I have everything I've ever wanted now. I have you. It's time I started to relax and enjoy life."

"Your life is with me, love," Nick said. "We're definitely going to enjoy it."

"Do you think we can start tonight?"

Nick wrinkled his nose. "What did you have in mind?"

"I'll race you home."

5. FIVE

"Granny, we need to talk," Maddie said, sitting down in the kitchen chair across from Maude the next afternoon.

"Is this where you tell me where babies come from?" Maude asked, her eyes wide. "I'm not sure if I'm ready for that."

Maddie pursed her lips, tilting her head to the side and forcing herself to remain calm even though there were times she legitimately wanted to shake her grandmother. Of course, the times she loved her far outweighed the bad times.

Maude sipped her tea, and Maddie didn't miss the flush of her cheeks. She had a feeling there was more than lemon zinger in the cup. "Where's the bourbon?"

"I have no idea," Maude said, taking another sip.

"You keep hiding it because you know I'm going to dump it out," Maddie said. "I'm onto you."

"I'm in my seventies, Maddie. I'm allowed to drink."

"I want you to live a really long time," Maddie said. "I don't think the bourbon is going to help my cause."

"Hey, I don't want to live a life that doesn't include bourbon," Maude said. "What did you want to talk about? Was that it? If it will make you feel better, I promise to relegate all of my drinking to the house this weekend."

"See, that makes me even more nervous," Maddie said. "What are you planning to do this weekend?"

"What do I do every weekend?"

"I have no idea," Maddie said. "You usually sneak around and stalk Harriet Proctor. You never give me the details, though. I'm a little worried to leave you here by yourself."

Maude rolled her eyes, making a comical face as she stuck her tongue out. "Oh, I have no idea what I'll do without you here policing my every move. I'll probably play with matches, run with scissors, and go swimming five minutes after I eat."

"I'm sorry," Maddie said, instantly contrite. "That's not fair. I don't mean to smother you. You're the only family I have left, though. It would kill me if something happened to you."

Maude's face softened. "Nothing is going to happen to me, Maddie girl," she said. "If it will make you feel better, though, I'll tell you what I'm doing. Tonight I'm going down to the fair. We're following Harriet around because we heard she's trying to influence another vote on the Pink Ladies council."

The Pink Ladies was the social group Maude belonged to. As far as Maddie could tell, the group essentially sat around and gossiped over tea and bourbon. She wasn't thrilled with the group, but since Maude needed constant stimulation, they were also a godsend.

Since Maude's mortal enemy, Harriet Proctor, announced her intention to infiltrate the group, it had been an "all hands on deck" situation for weeks. Maddie was weary of all the drama.

"That sounds ... fun," Maddie said. "You're not going to drive, right? I know you guys like to drink while you stalk."

"I'm not an idiot," Maude said.

"What are you going to do the rest of the weekend?"

"I'm having a card night on Saturday."

"Is that code for something?"

"Yes. It's code for having the Pink Ladies over so we can play euchre and drink more ... tea."

Maddie arched an eyebrow. "Tea?"

"Do we really have to do this?" Maude asked, sighing. "We both know I'm going to lie and say we're drinking straight tea. We both also know there's going to be whiskey in that tea. It's just so ... juvenile."

"Fine," Maddie said, giving in. "I'm just ... worried."

"Maddie, I don't think you're worried about me," Maude said. "I think you're nervous about going away with Nick for an entire weekend. You're going to be hanging around with people you don't know very well, and it's going to be a new experience for you.

"I think you're really worried about how *you're* going to handle this," she continued. "Instead of admitting that to yourself, though, you're focusing all of your attention on me."

"I ... you're right," Maddie said. "I'm sorry. I am worried about you, though."

"You're giving me an ulcer," Maude griped. "I'm going to be fine. You're going to be fine. Everyone is going to be fine. This is the first weekend since you came home where you haven't had something – like a murder, for crying out loud – hanging over your head. Can't you just enjoy it?"

Maddie furrowed her brow, taking in Maude's words and rolling them through her mind. "I hate it when you're right."

"I'm always right," Maude said. "Maddie, you're a young woman. You've got your whole life ahead of you. You're spending a romantic weekend with the man of your dreams. You're finally happy. Just ... enjoy it."

"How about we make a compromise?" Maddie suggested.

"What?" Maude was suspicious.

"I promise to enjoy my weekend if you promise to text me every morning ... just one sentence ... so I know you're okay. How about that?"

"Deal," Maude said, extending her hand.

Maddie shook it, grinning at her grandmother. "If you get arrested for stalking Harriet, though, make sure someone calls so we can come and bail you out."

"That would just be a wasted call," Maude said. "The judge won't grant bail on a holiday weekend. Trust me. I know."

Maddie frowned. "How do you know that?"

"I just do," Maude said. "Speaking of your fancy weekend, when are you leaving?"

Maddie glanced at the clock on the wall. "Soon," she said. "I should probably go and get our luggage from upstairs."

"That's what Nick is for," Maude said. "It's in the man handbook. They have to carry you over the threshold when you get married, they have to kill spiders in the tub, and they have to do the heavy lifting when you have a big suitcase. I don't make the rules. I just enforce them."

"Well, I'm a modern woman, Granny," Maddie said. "I'm more than capable of carrying two suitcases downstairs."

"Do what you want," Maude replied, nonplussed. "Just remember, I have enough wisdom for the both of us."

"I'll always remember that."

It took Maddie about five minutes to freshen up, and she was navigating the narrow staircase with her suitcase when something prickled the back of her neck. She felt as if she was being watched. She turned around quickly, expecting to find Olivia loitering in the hallway. The corridor was empty, though.

"Mom?"

"Did you say something, Maddie girl?" Maude asked, sticking her head through her bedroom doorframe.

"I ... were you just watching me?" Maddie asked, confused.

"I love you," Maude said. "I don't love you enough to find carrying a suitcase entertaining, though. Why?"

"I don't know," Maddie said, wrinkling her nose. "I felt as if someone was watching me."

"Maybe your mother is here."

"I don't see her," Maddie said. "She's generally not big on playing hide and seek."

"Maybe you're just tense," Maude suggested. "Do you want a cup of tea before you go? I'll bet the bourbon will settle your nerves."

"Thanks," Maddie said dryly. "I'd prefer to be sober when I get out to Aaron's house."

"Honey, I think there's going to be quite a bit of drinking out there this weekend," Maude said. "I know you're not used to people partying, but there's going to be drinking. Prepare yourself."

Maddie scowled. "I know people drink. I've been known to partake a time or two myself."

"Yes, but you never drink enough to get out of control," Maude said. "That defies the purpose of drinking if you ask me."

"I'll take that under advisement," Maddie said. "I ... ." There it was again. Maddie swiveled swiftly, turning her attention to the far end of the hallway. This time she was almost certain she saw a hint of wispy movement.

"What is it?" Maude asked. While she enjoyed messing with her granddaughter, she also knew how to read her face. Maddie was sensing something.

"I thought ... I thought I saw something down by my bedroom," Maddie said. "I ... I need to look."

"Be careful," Maude said. "Don't leave that suitcase in the middle of the stairs. Someone will trip over it."

"I'll take it down first," Maddie said, making up her mind quickly. "Do me a favor and stand right there. Don't move."

"I have nowhere to go."

After depositing her suitcase next to the front door, Maddie returned to the staircase. She was halfway up to the top when a keening wail assailed her ears. She swiveled again, preparing herself to find an angry spirit or ... something ... floating behind her.

The spot was empty.

"Granny?"

"What?"

"I ... something is in this house," Maddie said. "Can't you hear that?"

"You know I don't have the gift, Maddie," Maude said, appearing at the top of the stairs. "I ... ."

A filmy figure moved to the spot behind Maude, and before she realized what she was doing Maddie was racing up the steps. Maude pitched forward suddenly, her arms flailing forward. Maddie caught her before she could fall, using her body as a buffer to protect her fragile grandmother as they hit the ground at the top of the staircase.

"What was that?" Maude asked, breathless.

"There's a presence in the house."

"Your mother?"

"Mom would never try to push you down the stairs," Maddie said, shifting her head. "I ... where did it go?"

"I can't help you, Maddie," Maude said. "I don't know what to do."

"Sit here," Maddie said. "Keep your back to the wall." She got to her feet and peered around the corner. Nothing appeared to be out of the ordinary. Maddie stood there, willing the presence to return. After a few minutes, Maddie had pretty much convinced herself it was gone. When she turned back to Maude, she felt her body being snapped to the side as a force moved through her.

For a second, Maddie's mind was flooded with angry images – none of which she recognized. Then she was falling – and she was falling down the steps and toward certain doom.

NICK CAUGHT MADDIE IN MIDAIR, surprise washing over his features. He pressed her against his chest tightly, stunned and confused. "What the ... ?"

"There's something in the house," Maddie gasped, her heart pounding. "I ... Nicky."

She threw her arms around his neck, and even though he didn't understand what was happening, Nick cradled her close. "What's wrong, love?"

"There's something here," Maude said, peering around the corner. "It tried to knock me down the stairs and Maddie caught me. Then ... and I swear I'm not making this up ... I think I saw something run through her. It was just for a second, and it was like I was seeing it out of the corner of my eye, but it was definitely there."

"Stay there," Nick ordered. He carried Maddie down the steps and settled her on one of the chairs in the front of her store. He ran his hand down the side of her head, drawing her eyes up to his. "Are you okay?"

"I'm fine."

"I'm going up to get Maude," Nick said. "You stay here."

"I ... be careful."

"I'm always careful, love," Nick said. "You stay right here."

"I DON'T LIKE IT," Maddie said, her hands on her hips as she paced the kitchen. "We can't leave Granny here if there's something in the house."

"Are you sure it was a spirit?" Nick asked.

"I don't know," Maddie said. "That's what it felt like, and it when it ran through me I saw ... things."

"Like?"

"I don't know," Maddie replied, frustrated. "It was like I was seeing scenes from someone else's life. They were really brief clips, though. It all happened so fast. Whatever it was, though, it was angry. I'm sure of that."

Nick tugged on his ear, unsure. He believed Maddie implicitly. He was also in unfamiliar territory. "Do you want to cancel our weekend?"

"I ... ." Maddie broke off, worrying her bottom lip with her teeth.

"That's not going to happen," Maude said. "I want you guys to have your weekend. I'll be fine."

"No," Maddie said, immediately shaking her head. "I won't leave Granny in this house without knowing if something is here."

"Is it possible it was just one visit?" Nick asked. "Could the spirit have been ... I don't know ... drawn to you?"

"It's happened before," Maddie acknowledged.

"Do they usually stick around?"

"Actually ... no. It could've been a drive by."

"See, I'm fine," Maude said.

"There's always a first time for everything," Maddie said. "That spirit could've killed Granny on the stairs."

Nick rubbed the back of his neck thoughtfully. "Okay, how about everyone agree to a compromise? Maude, would you be willing to stay with one of your Pink Ladies for the weekend?"

Maude nodded without hesitation.

"If Maude promises to stay out of the house until we come back, will that make you happy? That would leave the house empty for several days. If a spirit is here, it will probably give up when it realizes no one is coming back."

Maddie wasn't thrilled with the suggestion, but since she couldn't think of anything better to do, she found herself nodding. "As long as Granny promises to stay out of the house until we get back, I'll agree to it."

Nick turned to Maude expectantly. "Do you promise?"

"I promise."

"Do you really promise? This isn't going to be one of those times where you say one thing and do the exact opposite, is it?" Nick pressed.

"No," Maude said. "I actually don't want to stay here right now. That whole thing freaked me out."

"Okay," Nick said. "I'm going to help Maude upstairs to pack. You're staying down here, Mad. I'm going to grab my suitcase while Maude is in her bedroom and bring it down. Then we're going to load everything up and get out of here.

"Hopefully we'll luck out and this will all blow over by the end of the weekend," he said.

"What if we don't luck out?" Maddie asked, her sea-blue eyes wide.

"Then we'll tackle that together when we get back," Nick said. "We're a family now, people. No one is doing anything alone."

6. SIX

"Oh, wow," Maddie said, exhaling heavily as Nick pulled onto the winding driveway that led up to the Denton mansion.

Blackstone Bay was a kitschy town, heavy on personality and light on modern conveniences – like big box stores and movie theaters. In essence, the town was small on style and big on heart. Still, many of the homes that spotted the hills and fields were impressive. Numerous affluent people chose Blackstone Bay to retire in, and the houses tended to reflect that.

Aaron Denton's familial home put every other house in the area to shame. In addition to the proximity to the river, the house boasted three floors, servants' quarters in the basement, two full libraries, a ballroom, and actual turrets. Maddie was in love at first sight. It was like she was visiting a castle.

Nick kept one eye on the road and the other on her face as he purposely slowed his approach so Maddie would have time to soak it all in. "Impressive, huh?"

"I just ... I've only read about places like this," Maddie said, leaning forward. "It's like we're in a fantasy book and this is our castle."

Nick smirked. "Does that mean I can call you my princess all weekend?"

"You can call me whatever you want," Maddie said. "Although … ." She broke off, shifting her eyes back out the window.

There was no way Nick was going to let that go without commenting. "Although what?"

"I don't want to tell you. You'll think I'm being schmaltzy."

"I happen to like you schmaltzy," Nick said. "Tell me. It's going to drive me nuts if you don't."

"I like it when you call me 'love.'" Maddie kept her face turned turned away from his. "It makes my heart flop when you say it. I can't explain it, and I know you're going to tease me about it, but there it is."

After a few moments of silence, Maddie finally risked a look back in Nick's direction. He was focused on the road as he pulled into one of the parking spots on the circular drive, but Maddie sensed something was on his mind.

"What are you thinking?"

"I'm thinking I love you," Nick said. He put his truck in park and shifted on the seat so he could face her. "You are my love. I don't think it's schmaltzy that your heart flops. Mine does every time I look at you."

"You look at me all the time," Maddie said, her expression rueful. "You must think you're constantly having a heart attack."

"Sometimes I do," Nick said. "I have to remind myself that this real, that I'm not dreaming, and that you are really mine. I never thought it was possible to be this happy, love. Never doubt that."

Maddie leaned over and gave him a soft kiss, promises of fun for later on her lips. Nick cupped the back of her head and held her steady for a moment, relishing their moment of privacy, and then he released her. "Do you want to call Maude now that we're up here to make sure she's settled?"

"How did you know I was thinking that?"

"I know you, Mad. It's okay. I want to make sure she's still at Beverly's house, too. I don't trust her not to go back. As it stands, I don't think it would hurt us to go for a drive a couple times this weekend ... and just happen to drive past the house."

Maddie smiled. "Thank you for understanding."

"Why wouldn't I understand?"

"You shouldn't have to deal with stuff like this," Maddie said. "It's not your fault that I'm so ... weird."

Nick sighed, exasperated. "You're not weird. You're special. I've known you were special since the day I met you. I had no idea how special until recently, but if you think I'm ashamed of you, then we're going to have a problem. I couldn't be prouder of you if you saved a busload of kids from falling off of a cliff."

"That's a weird comparison."

"Maybe I'm the weird one," Nick suggested. "Have you ever considered that?"

"Just every morning when I catch you singing Beyonce songs in the shower."

Nick flicked her ear. "Call Maude. I want to be able to enjoy the rest of our evening, and you're not going to relax until you talk to her. I'll grab our stuff."

"WELCOME TO MY HOME," Aaron said, gesturing widely and bowing as he ushered Maddie and Nick into the house. "It's ostentatious and over the top, but my mother can't do anything like a normal person, so it is what it is."

"It's beautiful," Maddie said. "I love the turrets."

"She wants to be a princess," Nick said, winking at Aaron.

"Is she going to make you wear tights and put a glass slipper on her foot?"

"Only when we're alone in our bedroom tonight."

"You know I can hear you, right?" Maddie asked.

"I'm not trying to be subtle, love," Nick said.

"You guys are the first ones here, although Brian and Max are supposed to be here already. Max said something about going on a beer run before he gets out here. I explained that my father has more liquor in this house than we could ever go through, and my parents leave it stocked when they're out of town like they are now, but old habits die hard."

Nick chuckled, and Maddie realized she was missing an inside joke. "What are you talking about?" she asked.

"We had a couple of parties up here back in the day," Nick explained. "Aaron was so terrified his father would notice the liquor was missing he paid a bum two towns over to buy for us."

"I don't remember you coming to parties up here," Maddie said.

Nick bit the inside of his cheek. "Oh, well, it was a long time ago."

"But ... ."

"It was after you took off for college and left him crying in his Gatorade," Aaron supplied. "Those first six months after you stopped talking to him were some wild times. He was going to classes in Traverse City, but we were partying here every weekend. Those were some great times.

"Do you remember those twins we picked up at that bar that one weekend?" Aaron continued, clearly missing the mortified look washing over Maddie's face. "We got so drunk we couldn't remember which one was which. I ended up sleeping with your date and you ended up sleeping with mine. They didn't realize it wasn't on purpose until the next morning. Man, were they pissed off."

"Mad," Nick said, searching for a way to explain.

"I'm so sorry," Maddie said, shaking her head. "I'm just so ... sorry."

"Mad, don't do that," Nick said, reaching for her.

"What did I do?" Aaron asked, confused.

"It's not you," Maddie said. "You didn't do anything. I did it."

"You didn't do it," Nick said. "Well, you did, but ... I'm sick of talking about it. I'm over it."

Maddie arched a confrontational eyebrow.

"Okay, I'm mostly over it," Nick said. "It hurt when you left and I lashed out. It's over now, though. We're together. I don't want to keep having to rehash this."

"I'm really sorry," Aaron said. "I didn't realize this was still a thing between you guys."

"It's not," Nick said. "We're over it."

"No offense, but it doesn't look like you're over it," Aaron said.

"We're mostly over it," Maddie corrected. "I still feel guilty, though."

"Well, if it's any consolation, he was miserable without you, Maddie," Aaron said. "The twins did help for a couple days, though."

"Shut up," Nick said, shaking his head. "Show us our room. We want to get unpacked before dinner."

"Well, since I've already stuck my foot in my mouth, how about I make it up to you?" Aaron suggested.

Nick narrowed his eyes. "What did you have in mind?"

"I WANT TO LIVE HERE," Maddie gushed, buzzing around the circular room excitedly. "We're sleeping in the top of a turret, Nicky. A turret. I really am a princess."

Nick reclined back on the bed, which was the first thing he tested, and rested his head on his hands as he watched Maddie excitedly explore the room. Since he was worried he'd upset her, Aaron rewarded her by assigning the couple one of the coveted turret suites. It boasted its own bedroom, sitting room, and bathroom. It was like a segregated apartment.

Nick didn't feel like a princess, but there was no way he was going to argue about the room assignment. Maddie was giddy, and that was exactly how Nick liked her.

"I wish I had a tiara for you," Nick said.

"I think that would be a bit much," Maddie said. "Especially for my outfit."

Nick grinned. "Come here, love."

Maddie bounced over to him, jumping onto the bed and landing next to him. "Are you going to let me sit on your throne?" She arched her eyebrow suggestively.

Nick barked out a coarse laugh, grabbing her around the waist and rolling on top of her. He kissed her lightly at first, deepening the exchange when he felt her body melt against his. After a few minutes of making out, he pulled back and brushed her hair away from her face so he could study it.

Her heart was pounding and she was flushed with excitement. In this exact moment, Nick had everything he'd ever wanted and he realized he'd never been happier. "I love you, Maddie."

"I love you, too," Maddie said. "Now ... come on ... worship me."

Nick grinned.

"Yes, your highness."

"**ARE** you sure I look okay in this dress?" Maddie smoothed the front of the floral frock down nervously.

"You look like every dream I've ever had about you, Maddie," Nick said, pressing his hand to the small of her back and prodding her down the stairs. Everyone was supposed to meet in one of the libraries for drinks before dinner, and Maddie was understandably nervous. Nick spent almost an hour trying to calm her. To him, she looked better than okay. Her long legs, tanned from hours under the sun, practically gleamed under the short dress, and her shoulders – which were one of his favorite things about her – were also on display.

In the back of his head, Nick knew it was wrong to parade Maddie around like she was a trophy. She was beautiful, though, and he was always proud to have her on his arm. Tonight was no exception. In fact, tonight she looked like something otherworldly, her blonde hair falling past her shoulders in honey-colored waves as the dress set off her blue eyes.

"I think the dress is too short," Maddie said.

"That dress makes your legs look a mile long," Nick said. "I love it. I'm going to buy Christy a house I love that dress so much."

Maddie pursed her lips, fighting the urge to laugh, and then gave in. "I think you're just a smooth talker when you want to be."

"I think so, too," Nick said. He gave her a short kiss. "Will you do me a favor?"

Maddie waited.

"Please try to relax," he said. "For me. I'll be right here. I'm sure people are going to ask some uncomfortable questions about why you left. They're going to ask how we got together. You don't have to answer them.

"Remember, Christy is going to be here," he continued. "If you just tell people to buzz off, they'll do it. They think they're joking. They don't understand that this is a touchier subject for us. They honestly don't. There's no one here that's going to purposely try to upset you."

"I know," Maddie said. "I'll agree to relax if you agree to do something for me."

Now it was Nick's turn to wait.

"Don't step over everyone and try to protect me," Maddie said. "It will be okay. If I need you, you'll know it. I want to have fun this weekend. You don't have to constantly be on alert to make sure I'm okay.

"As long as I have you, I'm always going to be okay," she said.

"You're always going to be okay then," Nick said. "There's nothing in this world you can do to shake me."

"Not even if I make a royal decree that you have to spend the weekend naked?" Maddie teased.

"Not even," Nick said, cupping the back of her head and kissing her deeply.

Maddie reached up and wiped the tinted gloss from his lips. "Okay. Let's do this. Do you know where this library is?"

Nick tilted his head to the side, listening. The sound of happy revelers wafted to their spot at the bottom of the staircase, and Nick slipped his hand around Maddie's and started to pull her in the direction of the voices.

"I'm kind of excited about dinner," he said. "I haven't eaten since breakfast. I was going to grab something at the house before we left, but then we had that whole thing with Maude."

"I'm hungry, too," Maddie said, fidgeting a little as Nick paused outside the library door.

"You look beautiful, Mad," Nick said. "Stop doing ... whatever it is you're doing."

"Stop hovering," Maddie countered. "Nothing is going to go wrong this weekend. Everything is going to be absolutely perfect."

Nick pushed the library doors open, greeting a few curious faces with a welcoming smile. The smile froze in place when he recognized two figures standing near the drink cart in the back of the room. "Oh, crap."

"I totally jinxed us," Maddie said.

"I ... why?"

Marla, her attention drawn to the new guests due to the sudden silence in the room, grinned evilly when she saw Maddie and Nick. At her side, Cassidy Dunham – Nick's ex-girlfriend – shift uncomfortably.

"I'm not joking," Maddie said. "I jinxed us. I'm not the princess, but there are my evil stepsisters. Someone had better call for my fairy godmother."

7. SEVEN

"Hey, we were starting to think you guys weren't going to come down." Aaron moved away from Marla and Cassidy and crossed the room. "Do you guys want a drink? Dinner won't be ready for at least a half hour."

"Um ... ." Nick glanced down at Maddie, unsure.

"A drink sounds great," Maddie said, forcing a smile and squaring her shoulders.

"Are you sure?" Nick asked. "We can go upstairs and pack if you want."

"Why would you pack?" Aaron asked. "Is something wrong?"

Nick shifted his gaze to Marla and Cassidy momentarily, and then back to Aaron. "I wasn't aware that Marla Proctor was invited," he said, keeping his voice low. "Her name was never brought up in all the conversations we had."

"I didn't invite her," Aaron said. "Apparently she and Max hooked up last night. He invited her."

"Max invited her to your house?" Nick asked dubiously.

"Max practically lived here with me when he was a kid," Aaron said. "It's kind of his home, too. I don't understand why this is a problem."

"It's not," Maddie said.

"No, it is," Nick countered. "We've had a few ... problems ... with Marla over the past two months. She's been less than welcoming to Maddie."

"She's a bitch," Aaron said, not missing a beat. "She's always been that way. Can't you just ignore her?"

"It's not just her," Nick said. "I ... um ... ."

"Okay, you're going to have to spit it out," Aaron said. "I'm not a mindreader."

"You don't need to be," Christy said, slipping between him and Maddie and handing the willowy blonde a glass of wine. "Drink up, Maddie. I think you're going to need something to take the edge off."

"Will you tell me what's going on?" Aaron asked.

"Well, let's see," Christy said. "How can I explain this in a way you'll understand?"

"Try English."

"When Maddie came back to town, Nick was involved with someone else," Christy said.

"Of course he was. He had a six-month cycle," Aaron said. "What? My mom keeps me up on all the gossip. Since she's only here six months out of every year, I have no idea how she keeps up on everything twelve months out of the year, but she does.

"Trust me. I know about Nick's cycle," he said. "I was actually pretty impressed with it. I tried to implement it into my own dating life, but I found I was the one who kept getting dumped. I'm starting to think it's me."

Maddie pursed her lips to keep from laughing. Aaron was a lot wittier than she remembered.

"Not everything is about you," Christy said, patting his arm. "Anyway, Nick was just getting ready to end his cycle when Maddie breezed back into town. Since everyone was waiting for him and Maddie to throw down and get busy in the middle of town, Nick decided not to break up with his girlfriend right away."

"Why?"

"Because he didn't want everyone in town assuming it was because of Maddie," Christy said.

"When did Blackstone Bay turn into a soap opera?" Aaron asked.

"I'm pretty sure it was 1985," Christy replied, not missing a beat. "Anyway, Nick and Maddie talked over their issues, and Nick realized he had to be with her or he was going to explode, but he still had that pesky girlfriend to deal with."

"You never could just tell a story in a hundred words or less," Aaron grumbled.

Christy ignored him. "The girlfriend figured out Nick was going to break up with her and proceeded to hide from him to try and put it off," she said. "Nick finally found her and dropped the hammer, and then he and Maddie got together the next day."

"So? That sounds like a happy ending to me," Aaron said, nonplussed.

"The ex-girlfriend in question is the woman Marla brought as her plus-one this weekend," Christy said.

"Oh," Aaron said, casting a look at Cassidy over his shoulder. The auburn-haired woman was staring at the small group with a dark look on her peaches-and-cream face. "Why couldn't you just say that from the beginning?"

"You would have missed a lot without the dramatic retelling," Christy said. "I'm sure you can understand that Maddie and Nick aren't comfortable around Cassidy and Marla. Marla has been going out of her way to stir the pot because she's always had issues with Maddie."

"It's called jealousy," Aaron said. "She's also always had a crush on Nick. I'll just bet she didn't tell Cassidy that little tidbit. How did my mother miss all of this when she was giving me the gossip last week?"

"I don't know," Christy said. "It was the talk of the town."

"I don't doubt it." Aaron looked back at Marla and Cassidy again. "I'll handle this."

"Wait," Maddie said, grabbing his arm to still him. "What are you going to do?"

"I'm going to kick them out."

"Don't do that."

"Why not?" Nick asked, making a face.

"That's just going to let them think they got to us," Maddie said. "I'm tired of having to change the way we act when they're around. Maybe we should make them adjust to us for a change."

"Are you sure you're up for that?" Nick asked.

"Of course she is," Aaron said. "Look at her. She looks like a Victoria's Secret model. Why would she care what the bitter twosome think?"

"She's sensitive," Nick said.

"Nicky," Maddie warned.

"What?"

"Stop trying to protect her," Christy answered for Maddie. "She'll be fine. I'm here. You're here. If Marla gets out of hand there's a river right out the back door for me to drown her in."

"I'm still not sure," Nick said, rubbing the back of his neck. "I thought we were going to get a chance to relax this weekend. Marla and Cassidy are anything but relaxing."

"Hey, man, if this Cassidy chick can't understand that you've been in love with Maddie since you were kids, that's on her," Aaron said. "Everyone in town knew about your dating schedule. I'm sure a couple of those chicks thought they were going to be the ones to break the cycle. It's not your fault they deluded themselves."

"Listen, I'm not particularly proud about what I did to Cassidy," Nick said. "She has a right to be angry ... at me. She tends to go after Maddie, though."

"Maddie already won the game," Aaron said. "Quite frankly, it was always rigged in her favor. I think this weekend could be a great way for you all to talk about things on neutral ground and get all your issues out in the open."

"That sounds like a good idea," Maddie said.

"That sounds like a terrible idea," Nick argued.

Maddie glanced at Christy for support.

"Oh, Maddie, it's a terrible idea," Christy said. "I can't wait to watch it, though. I'm still rooting for Marla to get doused in the river."

"We all are," Aaron said. "We'll make that our weekend pool."

"Good idea."

Nick sighed, but when Maddie squeezed his hand reassuringly, he gave in. "I guess we're staying," he said. "I'm reserving the right to put an end to this the second I feel like it's getting out of hand, though."

"Dude, if it gets that far I'll toss Marla out myself," Aaron said. "I figure one more night with her is all Max is going to be able to take. He said he liked the sex. It was her insistence on talking afterward that irritated him."

Nick grinned. "Okay. I need a drink if I'm going to be expected to make small talk with Marla and Cassidy, though."

"I guess it's good Max bought out the liquor store then," Aaron said. "Something tells me we're all going to need a bunch of drinks before this night is over with."

"SO, MADDIE, I was sorry to hear about your mom." Lauren Bishop brushed a strand of her dark hair behind her ear and fixed Maddie with a sympathetic look from across the dinner table. "I always liked Olivia. Last time I was in town, I guess it was two years ago now, she gave me a great reading at one of the fairs. She told me I was going to be rich and famous."

"Are you rich and famous?" Marla asked, making a face.

"No."

"It doesn't sound like a very good reading then, does it?"

Lauren placed her tongue in her cheek and narrowed her eyes in Marla's direction. "I see you're exactly the same as you were in high school. You're even wearing the same training bra if I'm not mistaken."

"What's going on?" Maddie whispered, leaning over so only Christy could hear her. "Does Lauren dislike Marla? I thought they were friends."

"They were friends junior year," Christy said. "Senior year Marla slept with Lauren's brother, and when he broke up with her, she told the girl he took to prom that he knocked her up. The rumor got back to Lauren's mom and it was a whole big thing. Then, the day before graduation, Lauren beat the crap out of Marla and Marla had to go to graduation with a black eye."

"How do you know all of this?"

"I got an A in gossiping," Christy said. "You can imagine how disappointed I was when I found out I couldn't major in it in college."

"Ah." Maddie sipped from her glass of wine and then shifted her eyes to Nick. From all outward appearances he looked relaxed, although Maddie knew he was poised to spring into action. "Are you okay?"

"I'm fine, Mad," Nick said, slipping his arm around her shoulders and giving her a brief squeeze. "I'm actually enjoying Lauren taking Marla down a peg or two."

"You just want to see if they're going to wrestle."

"We all want to see that," Max said, leaning between the two of them and smirking. "Why do you think I invited Marla? I knew there was a chance one of the women here would wrestle her. I'm hoping it's in underwear and bras."

"Thank you for that visual, Max," Nick said, making a face.

"Hey, I think that sounds like an awesome visual," Brian said, winking from across the table.

"What are you guys talking about down there?" Aaron asked from the head of the table.

"We were talking about ... how great this house is," Maddie lied.

"Actually, we were wondering how long it would be before Marla pissed off one of the ladies here enough to get the wrestling going," Max replied, guileless.

"We've got a pool going," Aaron said.

Marla's gaze bounced between Max and Aaron, her eyes slits as she decided how angry she should be at the suggestion.

"Maddie, you reopened your mom's shop, didn't you?" Lauren asked, directing the conversation back to a safer topic.

"I did," Maddie said. "It's been going pretty well. Although, we have construction going on upstairs and in the garage, so it has kind of been a pain to have customers in there with all that noise. I'm going to be so happy when everything is finished."

"Oh, I've always loved your house," Lauren said. "It's beautiful. I hope to be able to afford a Victorian of my own one day down the road. What are you having done?"

"We're turning the garage into an apartment for Granny," Maddie said. "Then I'm having the floors buffed in the master suite."

"We're upgrading the bathroom, too," Nick added. "It was pretty obsolete. We're having one of those garden tubs put in, and we're having the whole thing repainted."

Lauren lifted her perfectly manicured eyebrows. "We?"

"I'm moving in with Maddie," Nick said.

"That was quick," Max said, settling in the chair beside Marla.

"Very quick," Marla griped, making a face. "Some people might even call it rude it was so quick."

"What people?" Brian asked. "They're in love. They want to live together. I don't see who it's hurting. If Maude is fine moving into the garage, I don't think anyone else should care."

"Yes, I'm sure that poor old lady is perfectly fine being shuffled off into the garage," Marla said.

"Poor old lady?" Aaron laughed dryly. "Maude Graves doesn't do what she doesn't want to do."

"It was actually her idea," Maddie said. "She's been having trouble getting up and down the stairs, although she hates admitting it. My mother had plans to do the same thing before she died. I do love the house, but I never realized how dangerous those stairs could be for someone who is elderly."

"That's a convenient excuse," Marla said.

"Shut up, Marla," Christy said. "Unless someone invited you to act as a house designer for Maddie and Nick, you should probably keep your trap closed."

"You shut up, Christy."

"No, we all want you to shut up, Marla," Lauren said. "Why don't you let the adults talk for a few minutes?"

Marla crossed her arms over her chest, irritated. "I don't like being talked to like this."

"Then shut up," Max said, keeping his attention on Maddie and Nick. "What are you going to do with your house, Nick?"

"I'm selling it to my brother," Nick replied. "His house is on the market right now. He thinks he'll be ready to move six weeks from now. I wanted to keep the place in the family because I love to fish out there. This really is the best of both worlds."

"It sounds like you guys have it all planned out," Lauren said. "I'd love to see it when you're finished with the renovations."

"Whenever you want," Maddie said, smiling.

"When are you officially moving in, Nick?" Aaron asked.

"Technically I'm not moving in until the master bedroom is done," Nick said. "We spend every night together, though, so it's not like it will be a big change."

"You guys seem happy," Brian said. "It only took you ... what ... twelve years to admit you were madly in love with each other? That must be some sort of record."

"It doesn't matter how long it took them," Christy said. "It just matters that they finally got all the obstacles out of their way and admitted they were soul mates." It took Christy a moment to realize what she'd said, and she cast an apologetic look in Cassidy's direction. "I didn't mean that the way it sounded."

"It's fine," Cassidy said, waving her hand stiffly. "I'm used to hearing how I was the last obstacle to Maddie and Nick's happily ever after. I'm not embarrassed about being dumped in the dirt and treated like crap at all."

"You tell them," Marla said, spurring her on.

Nick and Maddie exchanged a brief look.

"So, where is that dinner?" Nick asked.

8. EIGHT

"I can't believe how close the river is to the back of the house," Maddie enthused, slipping her shoes off so she could wade into the slow-moving water.

Nick followed suit, bending over so he could roll up his pants before joining her.

"I would think this is against building regulations," he said, his gaze bouncing between the water and the back patio where everyone was milling about with cocktails. They were far enough away to speak freely, but they were close enough to still be considered part of the group. Nick was just happy to have a few minutes alone with his girl without Marla and Cassidy glaring at them like they'd been kicking kittens all night.

"I think, when you have as much money as Aaron's parents, you get around building regulations," Maddie said, her gaze focused on the river.

"Are you looking for a turtle?" Nick asked.

"No."

He didn't believe her. "Don't get that dress wet and ruin it," Nick warned. "I'll catch you a turtle tomorrow. We'll wear stuff that can get dirty and wet."

"I wasn't looking for a turtle," Maddie protested.

"You're always looking for a turtle," Nick said.

Maddie rolled her eyes and shifted her attention to the expansive lawn rolling down the other side of the river. "How did Aaron's family make their money? I don't think I even know what Mr. Denton does."

"They have family money," Nick said. "The grandfather was one of the initial investors in IBM, and Aaron's father continued the tradition by getting in early with Apple."

"Wow," Maddie said. "I guess they're smart when it comes to business."

"I would definitely agree," Nick said. "Still, as cool as this house is, I like the idea of something a little smaller. I like knowing that when I call your name you'll be able to hear me. The same goes for when we have kids. Can you imagine trying to wrangle little ones in this house?"

"I can barely imagine wrangling little ones in our house," Maddie replied.

"I guess it's good we don't have to worry about that for a little bit, isn't it?" Nick's question was pointed. He knew Maddie was worried he was anxious for kids, even though nothing could be further from the truth. "I'm happy it's just going to be the two of us for the next few years, Mad. We can have kids, but we don't need them right away."

"I know," Maddie said. "I just like dreaming sometimes. Is that so wrong?"

"No, love," Nick said, grinning. "I like dreaming, too. The thing is, we're already living our dream come true, so try to enjoy it."

"Then find me a turtle," Maddie said.

"I knew you were looking for a turtle," Nick grumbled.

"THEY REALLY LOOK HAPPY," Lauren said, sipping her martini and settling next to Christy as she watched Nick and Maddie cavort in the water. "I always knew they were destined to be together, but they're really adorable."

"They're so sugary sweet it's sickening sometimes," Christy said. "Can you tell I'm jealous?"

"I'm jealous, too," Lauren said. "Every little girl dreams of finding the perfect man. Maddie actually found hers."

"It's too bad they couldn't have realized that back in high school," Aaron said, joining them. "They would probably already be married and have kids if they hadn't been so scared to admit how they felt back then."

"I think they're better off," Christy said.

"Why do you say that?"

"Think about it," Christy said. "We were all idiots when were eighteen years old. If they'd tried to make it work then, they probably would've failed and missed their chance. Now they're both older, they're both more mature ... things just fit together perfectly for them."

"Other than the woman they crushed on the way to their own happiness," Marla said.

Christy ran her tongue over her teeth as she turned to Marla. Cassidy was standing next to her, and the look on her face was murderous. "Can't you just let it go, Marla? Everyone in this town knew Nick was pining for Maddie. No one is saying what happened to Cassidy was right – especially Nick – but it's over and done with. It's not like anything is going to change. Maddie and Nick are happy. They're not going to break up."

"Until the six-month mark when Nick gets bored and decides he's ready to move on and start another cycle," Marla said.

"Oh, please," Max scoffed, brushing past Marla and sitting in one of the patio chairs. "Nick is never going to get bored with Maddie. Those two were always in their own little world. No one else was even allowed to visit their world."

"I thought Nick was popular," Cassidy interjected. "Wasn't he on the football team? How was he locked away in a world with Maddie if he was part of the popular clique?"

"Nick was on the football team, the basketball team, and the base-ball team," Aaron replied. "Those were things he did, though. Maddie came to each game and cheered him on, and then as soon as it was over, they left together.

"Nick didn't go to team parties, and he really didn't hang out with us that much off the field or court," he continued. "All he cared about was running around the woods with Maddie. I swear, I always thought they were out there doing it. I was so disappointed when I spied on them and found out they really were just wishing on stars."

"I spied on them, too," Brian said, chuckling. "I wanted to see Maddie naked something fierce. I still wouldn't mind seeing Maddie naked."

"I wouldn't say that when Nick can hear," Max said.

"You wouldn't say what when Nick can hear?" Nick stepped up onto the patio, his gaze busy as it moved from face to face.

"We weren't talking about you," Lauren said hurriedly.

"Yes, we were," Christy said, knowing right away that lying was the wrong way to go. "We started out by saying how jealous we were of the two of you, and then Aaron and Brian admitted they snuck out to the woods behind Maddie's house to spy on you guys when you were in high school."

"Why?" Nick asked, confused.

"We thought you two were doing it," Aaron admitted sheepishly.

"They also wanted to see Maddie naked," Christy added.

"Brian wanted to see her naked," Aaron said, pointing. "I didn't. I'm not a pig."

Nick rolled his eyes. "You all wanted to see her naked," he said. "I'm not stupid. And, if you want to know the truth, it's fantastic and you have no idea what you're missing." He shuffled over to the drink cart and grabbed two beers. "She looks like a goddess without her clothes on."

Max snickered. "I knew it! She looks like a goddess with her clothes on. Nudity must be like Heaven where you two are concerned. Wait ... that makes it sound like I want to see Nick naked, doesn't it?"

"Don't worry, you're not the only one," Lauren teased.

Nick's cheeks colored. "You guys need to pick another activity," he said. "The gossiping is getting old."

"Then you and Maddie should stop being so cute," Lauren challenged.

"That's impossible," Nick said. "Maddie was born cute and she's going to die cute."

"I'm going to puke," Marla said.

"The bathroom is in the house," Aaron said, not missing a beat.

"Now, if you don't mind, I think I'm going to rejoin my girl in her turtle hunt," Nick said.

"Turtle hunt? Is that what she's doing?" Brian asked, leaning forward so he could study Maddie. "She's never going to catch a turtle sloshing around like that."

"She doesn't catch them," Nick said. "She finds them and then makes me catch them."

"Oh, you two are even cuter now," Lauren said. "You're like a PG-13 couple with model looks and hot kisses."

"How do you know the kisses are hot?" Nick challenged.

"Because I've seen the way you two look at each other," Lauren replied. "No one smolders that much without some payoff between the sheets."

"And I'm done here," Nick said, moving back toward the steps. "You guys are just ... too much."

The night sky split suddenly, a bright bolt of lightning flashing. A terrific rumble of thunder followed, loud enough to shake the patio.

"I didn't know it was going to storm," Lauren said, disappointed.

"We should probably move this party inside," Aaron said. "We're going to get wet in exactly thirty seconds."

"I need to get Maddie," Nick said, turning his head as the wind gusted. She was still by the water, but her eyes were fixed on a spot behind a nearby tree and her back was to him. Nick had no idea what she was doing, but something told him her attention had been drawn to something only she could see. "Take these inside for us," Nick said, handing the beers to Christy.

"What is she looking at?" Max asked, tilting his head to the side.

"There's probably some deer out there," Aaron said. "They've been coming closer to the house over the past few days."

"I'm sure that's it," Nick said, exchanging a quick look with

Christy. Both of them knew Maddie's attention was more likely fixed on something supernatural.

"Let's go inside," Christy said, jumping into action. "Nick is fully capable of collecting Maddie."

"I'll be right back," Nick said.

MADDIE STARED AT THE GHOST, conflicted. The woman looked to have been in her early forties when she died, her dark hair shot through with gray, and the beginnings of some heavy lines colliding in the corners by her eyes. Her eyes were an odd color, more gray than blue or green, and she looked like she was wearing some sort of uniform – although Maddie couldn't identify it.

"You can see me, can't you?" The woman was studying Maddie with the same intensity as Maddie was looking at her.

"Yes," Maddie whispered, making sure to keep her back to the patio so no one could see her lips moving. "Who are you?"

"Who are you?"

"My name is Maddie Graves."

"Are you Maude's daughter?"

Maddie stilled, surprised. "I'm her granddaughter. Do you know my grandmother?"

"She shouldn't be old enough to be a grandmother," the ghost mused. "Olivia is still so young. I didn't even know she was pregnant."

Maddie was confused, although she had a feeling she was nowhere near as confused as the spirit. "What year do you think it is?"

"It's ... um, I don't know. Time doesn't mean anything to me now."

Maddie pressed her lips together. "That's okay. Um ... did you die here?"

"Someone is coming," the ghost hissed, drifting to the side and hiding behind a tree.

Maddie turned, not surprised to find Nick moving in her direction.

"It's going to storm, Mad," Nick said. "We need to get inside."

"Umm ... okay." Maddie glanced back at the woman.

Nick didn't speak again until he was at Maddie's side and could keep his voice low. "Who are you talking to?"

"There's a ghost here," Maddie said, tilting her head. "I ... how did you know I was talking to someone? Does everyone up there think I'm talking to myself?"

"Calm down," Nick said, rubbing her back and leaning closer. He wanted prying eyes to think they were being romantic. "Everyone thinks you're looking at deer and that's going to be your story when we go back inside. It's fine. No one besides Christy suspects anything."

"Are you sure?"

"I'm sure, Mad. Tell me about the ghost. Do you recognize her?"

"No," Maddie said. "She hasn't told me her name. Do you want to tell me who you are?"

The woman remained silent, her eyes flooding with suspicion as they fixed on Nick.

"She knew Granny, although she thought I was her daughter," Maddie said.

"She thought you were Olivia?" Maddie and her mother shared mesmerizing eyes and lithe figures, but Olivia's coloring was much darker than Maddie's. Nick had never met anyone who confused the two women.

"No, she just asked if I was Maude Graves' daughter," Maddie replied. "She has no idea what year it is. In her mind, Granny shouldn't be a ... well ... granny, yet."

"I'm sure Maude will be happy to hear that," Nick said, kissing Maddie's cheek. Another bolt of lightning ripped through the air, followed quickly by a menacing rumble of thunder. "Love, I'm willing to stay out here with you if you think it's necessary, but that's going to be hard to explain. Do you think we can put this conversation off until tomorrow and get inside before it starts to rain?"

"I ... ." Maddie broke off, worrying her bottom lip with her teeth. She wasn't particularly fond of abandoning people – or spirits – in need. This woman was lost in time. She was definitely in need.

"Go," the woman said finally. "It's not safe out here ... especially after dark."

"What do you mean by that?"

"Beware of the shadows," the woman said, glancing at Nick one more time. "Be careful who you trust."

She blinked out of existence, and when the thunder rolled again, Maddie slipped her hand into Nick's. "We should go now. She's gone."

"We'll talk about it upstairs," Nick said, pushing Maddie in front of him and keeping her body close to his as he sheltered her from the rain, which was starting to fall. "We'll tell everyone we're going to bed early."

"That doesn't seem fair to you."

"Mad, as long as I'm with you, everything is fine," Nick said. "Never doubt that. Now, come on, love. This looks like it's going to be one heck of a storm."

9. NINE

Maddie woke the next morning with Nick's body spooning against her backside. His face was resting in the hollow between her shoulder and neck, and he was breathing in an even rhythm as his heart beat in sync with hers.

This was her favorite part of the day. She loved waking up earlier than him because it allowed her the opportunity to bask in their shared warmth and just ... think. She didn't think about anything in particular. Sometimes she dreamed about their future, and sometimes she got lost in memories of their past. Each morning was spent thinking about him, though. He was her favorite daydreaming subject.

"I can hear the gears in your mind grinding from here," Nick teased, brushing his lips against her jaw.

"Did I wake you up?" Maddie asked, disappointed.

"Why does it sound like you wish I was still asleep?"

"I don't know," Maddie hedged. "I just like waking up before you. You're usually up before me during the week, so on the weekends I like to just ... lay next to you and listen to you breathe. Don't you dare laugh at me for that, either."

"I do the same thing, Mad."

"You do?"

"I like to look at you in the morning," Nick said. "You look like an angel when you sleep."

"Does that mean I look like the Devil when I'm awake?"

"Only when you're doing something naughty," Nick said, splaying his fingers against Maddie's flat midriff and pulling her tighter against his body. "How did you sleep?"

"Soundly," Maddie said. "I know it's weird, but thunderstorms always knock me out."

"I like thunderstorms, too," Nick said. "As long as they're not too bad, that is. I don't like it when they knock the power out."

"I'm betting this place has a generator," Maddie said.

"I'm betting they have a backup generator for the generator," Nick said. "What time is it?"

Maddie glanced at the clock on the nightstand. "It's almost seven. We should probably get up. Didn't Aaron say breakfast would be served at eight?"

"He did," Nick said. "We don't need to eat breakfast if you don't want to, though. We can do something else if you'd rather spend the day in bed."

Maddie smirked, moving her hand down so she could trace his fingers. "What did you have in mind?"

"Well, I thought I'd start with a little of this." Nick licked the ridge of her ear, causing her to shudder. "Then I thought I would do a little of this." Nick kissed her neck and then lightly sucked the skin into his mouth. "And then I thought ... ." He was interrupted by the sound of his stomach growling.

Maddie giggled. "I think there are two ideas warring for supremacy in that godlike body of yours."

"Mad, where you're concerned there is no war," Nick said. "You've already won every battle there is."

"What if we compromise?"

"I'm listening."

"I was thinking that we could get up and take a shower together – and do whatever comes naturally in there – and then we would still have plenty of time to get ready for breakfast so you can fuel up," she said.

"Sold," Nick said, playfully patting her rear. "If you're a really good girl, I'll even wash your back while we're in there."

"I'll race you to the shower."

"HOW DID YOU TWO SLEEP?" Christy asked, reaching for a croissant as she glanced at Maddie and Nick. "Given how you're glowing, I'm guessing sporadically."

"What do you mean?" Maddie asked, furrowing her brow.

"Oh, you're such a good girl," Christy said, pinching her friend's cheek as she teased her. "You don't even know when I'm being a terrible friend sometimes."

Nick watched Maddie, waiting for her to get what Christy was talking about. When she finally did, her cheeks flushed with color. "And there it is," he said.

"You really need to explain the concept of sarcasm and suggestive innuendo to her when you have time, Nick," Christy said.

"I thought that was part of your curriculum," Nick replied, reaching for his own croissant. "I am starving."

"That's because you worked up an appetite," Christy said.

"You've got that right."

"You two are going to give me an ulcer," Maddie grumbled.

"I keep trying," Christy said.

"So, what does everyone want to do today?" Aaron asked. "I figured we could go to the fair for a couple hours, or we could just hang around the house. We have a basketball court if anyone wants to do that, or we have tennis courts. There's a pool, too."

"I want to see the family cemetery," Marla said, speaking for the first time that morning. She didn't look happy when she descended the stairs twenty minutes before, and if the eye daggers she was lobbing in Max's direction were any indication, the previous evening hadn't gone as planned.

"You want to see the family cemetery?" Aaron asked, surprised. "It's not much to look at. It's just a cemetery."

"How many plots are there?" Nick asked, curious despite himself.

"It wasn't always the family plot," Aaron explained. "It was the town cemetery when Blackstone Bay was first founded, but once my family bought the property, the town opted to start their own cemetery and our plot just became a spot to plant family members."

"Nice," Lauren said, sipping from her glass of orange juice.

"Can you think of a better way to put it?"

"Can't you just say you put people to rest there? Cemeteries always creep me out."

"I like them." The words were out of Maddie's mouth before she realized what she was saying. "I mean ... um ... I find them interesting."

Multiple sets of eyes shifted until they landed on her.

"What? I like to look at the headstones and sculptures," Maddie said. "There's something beautiful about putting someone in their eternal resting place."

"You've got a morbid streak, don't you?" Christy asked.

"Leave her alone," Nick said, patting Maddie's knee under the table before stealing a slice of bacon from her plate. "I think cemeteries are cool, too."

"We should all go together," Marla suggested.

Nick made a face. "Marla, the only time I want to be in a cemetery with you is if I'm going to your funeral."

"Nicky," Maddie scolded.

"I'm sorry," Nick said, instantly contrite. "That was a horrible thing to say. I actually don't wish you dead, Marla."

"Thank you."

"I just wish your tongue would fall out," Nick said.

Everyone at the table snickered except for Marla and Maddie. Marla was angry, for obvious reasons, and Maddie didn't want to stoke the fire of Marla's hatred.

"We can go to the cemetery," Aaron said. "I actually haven't been there in a few years. It is kind of cool. My great-grandfather built a mausoleum, mostly because he didn't want to be planted next to the common folk, but there are some cool sculptures and some of the tombstones are really old and ornate."

"That sounds fun to me," Max said. "Do you remember when we used to play hide and seek down there when we were kids?"

"I forgot how much time you used to spend out here," Lauren said. "Your mother worked here, right?"

"She did," Max said. "She loved this house. We lived in the servants' quarters for years before moving to our own apartment when I was a teenager, but Aaron's family never made me feel like I wasn't part of the family. I always thought it was so cool out here."

"You were part of the family," Aaron said. "You ate breakfast with me every morning, and a couple of years there you hauled in more Christmas presents than me."

"That was because your father was punishing you for snooping," Max said, laughing at the memory. "I still remember when he gave me your bicycle. I think that was because you told your cousin Santa Claus wasn't real. Man, your mother was hopping mad."

"My mother was always hopping mad," Aaron said. "I love her, but that woman grounded me more times than I can even remember."

"Maybe you deserved it," Christy suggested.

"No one deserves to be grounded as much as I was. I went two months without being able to leave the property one summer."

"Why do you think she did it?" Lauren asked.

"I think she liked it," Aaron said. "She got off on being mean. Hey, I'm not talking badly about my mother. There's no reason to look at me that way. My mother is proud of being mean. She puts it on her business cards."

Lauren giggled. "She once told me that she was going to cut all my hair off if I didn't make sure it stopped getting in my mouth when we were playing outside," she said. "She was always nice to me, but she did get off on scaring me, too."

"She was the only one in the house who hated me," Max said.

"She didn't hate you," Aaron argued.

"She did, too," Max said. "Don't bother lying. She always thought I was beneath you. It's fine. Don't worry about it. Everyone else in your family was great to me. I just learned at a really young age to make myself scarce when your mother was home."

"I guess it's good she wasn't home all that often," Aaron said. "Now that you mention it, though, I remember having a lot more fun when she was gone than when she was here."

"I don't remember your mother being anything but pleasant," Nick said. "I don't remember spending a lot of time around her, but she was always nice to me when I came out here."

"That's because she was scared of your mother," Aaron said. "My mother knew darned well that your mother could make her life hell on all those little town boards they were on together.

"My mother gained power through money, but your mother gained power through popularity," he continued. "My mother is a smart woman. She knew which type of power held more weight."

"How come I didn't know any of this was going on?" Maddie asked. "I must have been out of the loop."

"You just had your own loop," Christy said. "You spent all of your time with your mother, grandmother, and Nick. Your loop was pretty small."

"It was," Maddie conceded. "We had fun, though."

"We had a lot of fun," Nick said, tapping Maddie's plate. "If we're going to be wandering around all morning you need to eat your breakfast."

"Yes, Dad."

Nick scowled. "I hate it when you do that."

"I hate it when you tell me what to do," Maddie replied.

"Oh, good, they're finally going to fight," Marla said. "I was getting sick of them pretending things were always perfect."

Nick ignored her. "I'm not telling you what to do." He leaned forward and whispered something into her ear, and while no one could hear what he said, the gist of it was obvious when Maddie's face turned pink.

"Oh, look, Nick just convinced Maddie to eat her breakfast with promises of naughty fun later," Christy said, grinning.

"How did you know that?" Maddie asked, mortified.

"You just told me," Christy said.

"I hate it when you do that," Maddie muttered.

"I hate it when you forget that I do that," Christy said. "Well, actually, that's not true. I love it when you forget I do that because that's always how I get you to own up to all the dirty stuff I know you and Nick are doing."

Nick reached around Maddie and flicked Christy's ear. "Don't embarrass her."

Christy jerked her head away from Nick, rubbing her ear ruefully. "I hate it when you do that."

"Then stop making me do it," Nick said.

"Everyone is in a fun mood this morning," Brian said, rolling his eyes.

"I hate mornings," Marla said. "They make me grumpy."

"I think that's just your personality," Christy suggested.

"Me, too," Lauren chimed in.

The conversation was quickly veering into dangerous territory.

"So, we've all agreed to go down to the cemetery together?" Aaron asked, hoping to change the subject.

"I'm game," Brian said. "I've never seen it. After that, though, I want to have a basketball tournament this afternoon. There are four of us. We can have even teams."

"That sounds fun," Max said, turning his attention to Nick. "Does that sound okay to you?"

Nick shrugged. "I'm up for going to the cemetery, but I'll have to think about playing basketball."

"Why? Did you forget how to play?"

"No," Nick said. "I just promised Maddie I would spend the afternoon catching her a turtle."

"Don't you do that every weekend?" Christy asked.

"So?"

"So you should play basketball with the boys so I can gossip with Lauren and Maddie," Christy said, filling in the blanks for him.

"What are you going to gossip about?" Nick asked curiously.

"You."

"I hate it when you do that," Nick grumbled.

10. TEN

"Wow," Christy said, pushing her red hair away from her face and studying the cemetery plot with wide eyes. "I know you said that some of the townspeople were put to rest here, but I wasn't expecting this."

"It's not that big," Aaron said. "I think there are only three hundred people here total. When you think about it, that's nothing."

"That doesn't seem like nothing to me," Cassidy said. "The idea of three hundred people being buried in my yard totally freaks me out." She shuffled a little closer to Nick, a move Maddie didn't miss. She also didn't comment on it. She didn't want to make a scene. "Don't you think that's freaky, Nick?" Cassidy asked, her eyes wide.

Nick glanced at her, unsure how to answer. Since ending their relationship Cassidy's moods swung wildly. One second she was angry and vengeful. The next she was a sobbing mess. He could never be sure which version of Cassidy he was going to get.

The truth was, and he had trouble admitting it even to himself, he didn't know much about the woman. When he started dating her, the only thing he knew was that she was pretty and amiable. When he'd been looking for people to date, Nick always picked moldable women who would be willing to let him set limitations on the relationship. Those limitations usually involved a maximum of two dates a week.

He never introduced the women to his family, and he always found a reason to get out of meeting their families. He drew clear lines in the sand. Despite all of that, Cassidy somehow believed they had a future. He still couldn't fathom it.

"I'm not scared of cemeteries," Nick said, moving away from Cassidy and sidling up behind Maddie. Her eyes were busy as she scanned the cemetery, and Nick knew exactly what she was looking for. He rested a hand on her hip to let her know he was there but he didn't otherwise distract her. "I've always enjoyed hanging out in them. When we were in middle school, Maddie once convinced me to spend the night in a cemetery because she saw it in a movie and thought it would be cool."

Christy laughed. "Did you?"

"I did," Nick said. "It was actually pretty fun. It was her idea, but she got scared in the middle of the night and crawled into my sleeping bag with me."

"Did you get to second base?" Max asked.

Nick tilted his head to the side, racking his brain. "Technically? Yes. I had no idea that's what was happening, though. I honestly thought my hand was on her stomach."

"Nice," Maddie said. "Is that a comment on how flat chested I was back then?"

"It's okay, Mad," Nick said. "By the time we hit senior year, I finally figured out you had boobs."

"You've told me this story," Maddie groaned.

"I haven't heard it," Max said. "Go on."

"No one wants to hear this story," Marla said.

"I do," Aaron said. "Shut up."

"It's not a big story," Nick said, tickling Maddie's ribs. "We were in the funhouse at one of the fairs and Maddie got scared and jumped into my arms. It just so happens that her boobs were smushed up against me. I hadn't realized how big they'd gotten until then, and after that, it was all I could think about. It was the best moment of my life ... until recently." He kissed Maddie's cheek to reassure her. "I've had better moments since."

"Oh, you're so romantic," Lauren said.

"Are you being sarcastic?" Nick asked. "I can't tell."

"Oh, no," Lauren said, rolling her eyes. "All women love hearing a good 'he touched my boob' story about their teenage years. It's like a dream come true."

Christy snickered.

"That's a terrible story," Aaron said. "I thought it was going to get way dirtier."

"I've decided that all men are pigs when they get together in little groups," Maddie said.

"You're coming to that party late," Christy said.

"Well, we're going to look around," Nick said, linking his fingers with Maddie's.

"You just want to get her alone because you're worried she's going to be mad at you," Max said. "You should let her get mad at you occasionally, my man."

"Why is that?"

"Because, if you think touching her boob when you were a teenager was great, wait until you get to have some righteous make-up sex."

"How do you know we haven't already done that?" Nick asked.

"Because you two are still in the honeymoon stage of your relationship," Max said. "It's pretty obvious you haven't fought yet. When it happens, you're going to think the world is ending until you make up. Then, when you make up, you're going to go out of your way to fight again just so you can repeat the experience."

Nick grinned as he glanced down at Maddie. "What do you think? Do you want to fight?"

"I think you should stay here and tell your funhouse story again," Maddie said, pulling away from him. "I want to look around."

"Alone?"

"I'll go with her," Christy said. "We wouldn't want to cut your teenage memories short."

Nick shifted slightly, considering the offer. He didn't want to leave Maddie alone, especially when he knew she was looking for a ghost.

Still, Christy was aware of Maddie's psychic gifts. She would stick close to her. He'd promised Maddie he wouldn't hover and this was the first test of his resolve. "Okay," he said, leaning over so he could give Maddie a quick kiss. "Have fun."

"DID YOU SEE A GHOST LAST NIGHT?" Christy asked as she walked along the cobblestone path with Maddie. "I saw you staring into the trees, and no matter what Aaron said, it didn't look like you were staring at deer to me."

"I did," Maddie said, glancing around to make sure no one was eavesdropping.

"Do you know who it was?"

"She didn't say," Maddie replied.

"Can you describe her?"

"She looked like she was in her forties. She had dark hair, but there was quite a bit of gray in it. She was wearing a weird little uniform."

"Like a maid's uniform?"

"No. I'm not sure how I would describe it. It was bluish white."

"Hmm. Did she tell you who she was?"

"No," Maddie said. "She seemed confused by her surroundings. She did know Granny, though, if you can believe that?"

"That means she died within the last fifty years or so, right?"

"She knew who my mother was, too," Maddie said. "She thought I was Granny's daughter at first, but then it was like she got caught in time. By the time Nick got back to me it seemed like she was scared."

"Well, I'm sure you'll find her," Christy said. "Just be careful when you talk to her. Make sure no one can see you but Nick or me. If Marla catches you talking to a ghost you're never going to hear the end of it."

"I'm not sure I care what Marla thinks," Maddie said.

"Since when?"

"Since ... I don't know," Maddie said. "It's not one of those overnight things. It's more of a gradual thing. The more time I spend around her, the more I realize that she's just a genuinely unhappy person. It's not me that she hates. It's her circumstances."

"You're cute," Christy said.

"Meaning?"

"She hates you, Maddie," Christy said. "It's not because you're different, though. She hates you because you've gotten everything she's ever wanted. At first, she hated you because she wanted Nick and his relationship with you made it impossible for her to get him.

"Now she hates you because you swooped back into town and claimed Nick when she worked for years to get him to come around to her way of thinking while you were gone," she continued. "I think she honestly thought she could make him fall in love with her somehow."

"She doesn't really know Nick, though," Maddie pointed out. "I don't see how she could convince herself she has feelings for him when she can't see inside his heart."

"Oh, so schmaltzy," Christy said, mock clutching her heart.

"You know what I mean."

"I do," Christy said, sobering. "I also know you're using logic when you should be thinking with a cold pit that doubles as a heart. That's what Marla thinks with."

Maddie chewed on the inside of her cheek as she considered Christy's words. She'd learned that the woman was pretty savvy when it came to reading the human condition.

"Marla wants Nick because he was one of the big prizes in high school," Christy said. "She wanted him then because she thought it would cement her popularity. She was desperate to get him to notice her. The problem was she tried to get him to notice her by demeaning you. That's not the way to Nick Winters' heart."

"I guess I don't understand why she would hold onto that for so long," Maddie said. "High school was a long time ago."

"High school is forever for girls like Marla," Christy said. "Once you left town Marla convinced herself she had a chance with Nick. He was too depressed at first to bother with her, and then he was too smart to even consider it later. Trust me. Marla is the type of woman who would conveniently forget to take her birth control if she thought she could snag the right man."

"That's horrible."

"Marla is horrible," Christy said.

Maddie shifted her attention in the direction of the mausoleum, and when she did, her gaze fell on the ghost from the previous evening. She was floating by the door watching them.

"She's here," Maddie said, gripping Christy's hand.

"Who? Marla?"

"No. The ghost."

Christy followed the track of Maddie's eyes with her own, momentarily disappointed she couldn't see the ghost. "I wish your superpowers would transfer over to me. I want to see a ghost."

"It's not all it's cracked up to be."

"That's easy for you to say," Christy said. "Do you want to try and talk to her?"

"I don't know," Maddie said, letting her gaze wander around the cemetery. Nick and the other men were still standing in the center of the plot telling stories. Whatever Max was reenacting had them all in stitches. Lauren was kneeling next to an older tombstone, apparently intent on whatever she was reading. Cassidy and Marla were nowhere in sight. "Where did Cassidy and Marla go?"

"I have no idea," Christy said. "Maybe we got lucky and they headed back to the house."

"Will you do me a favor and keep an eye out for them? I'll try to talk to the ghost."

"I want to go with you," Christy protested.

"You can't even hear her."

"Fine." Christy crossed her arms over her chest. "You're lucky I'm such a good friend."

"I am lucky," Maddie sincerely replied. "You're the second best friend I've had my entire life."

Christy's face softened. "Go and help the ghost, you suck up," she said. "You're a good friend, too, and I want to help you if I can."

"Thanks," Maddie said. "Warn me if you see Marla and Cassidy show back up."

"I'm still hoping they fell in the river or something."

"HI," Maddie said, approaching the spirit carefully a few minutes later. "Are you ready to talk to me now?"

"You're still here."

"I am," Maddie said. "I ... do you think we could go inside and talk? It might make things easier."

Instead of answering the spirit floated through the door and disappeared to the other side. Maddie was taking that as a yes.

Maddie let herself into the mausoleum, being careful to leave the door propped open so she didn't inadvertently lock herself in. The ghost was waiting for her, the filtered light barely serving as a means to see the woman's filmy countenance.

"Can everyone in your family see and talk to ghosts?"

"Not everyone," Maddie said carefully. "My mother could. My grandmother, on the other hand, can't. Many of the women in my family have ... the gift. Not all of them, though. We have no idea why it skips certain generations."

"That's interesting," the woman said. "Before I died, I would've thought it was nifty to see ghosts."

"What about now?"

"Now I wish I could see anything but this place."

Maddie's heart went out to the woman. She'd been here a long time. Too long. She obviously longed to pass on. Maddie only hoped she would be able to help her with the process. "What's your name?"

"Rose. Rose Denton."

She was finally getting somewhere. "How are you related to Aaron?"

"He's my grandson, although I've never technically met him," Rose said. "I died long before he was born."

Maddie nodded, absorbing the information as she glanced around the mausoleum. She read the plaques, not stopping until she came to the name she was looking for. She moved toward it, resting her fingertips on the cold metal and tracing the elevated letters. "Is this you?"

"That's me. Rose Eloise Denton. Born April 12, 1927. Died December 12, 1970."

"How did you die?"

"Hard."

That wasn't really an answer, but Maddie didn't want to push the woman if she wasn't ready to expand. "If you're Aaron's grandmother, that means you died when his father was still relatively young. Did you have more than one child?"

"No, just the one."

"Do you spend a lot of time watching your family?"

"The house is empty a lot of the time," Rose said. "I watch them sometimes. Other times ... I just kind of exist. I'm not really thinking about anything, or remembering anything. I'm aware that life is going on without me. Of course, it felt like life was going on without me even when I was alive."

Sympathy for the woman bubbled up, although Maddie wasn't exactly sure why. She was clearly sad, but until she opened up, there was nothing Maddie could do to help her. "You know, if you tell me how you died, I might be able to help you move on."

"To where?"

'The other side," Maddie said. "I'm not sure what's waiting for you, but it has to be better than what you're living with here."

Rose considered the offer. "I'm not sure ... I don't ... ." She squared her shoulders, almost as if she'd been trying to decide how to answer, and finally made up her mind. "I was murdered."

Maddie opened her mouth to reply, a hundred different questions fighting for top billing on the tip of her tongue, but she didn't get a chance to ask any of them because the sound of the mausoleum door swinging shut assailed her ears instead.

That was when Maddie realized she'd made a terrible mistake. It seemed the only light in the room was filtering in through a small window at the top of the building – and the door, which had been propped open, cut off the bulk of the light when it slammed shut.

Now Maddie found herself plunged into virtual darkness, and she was trying really hard not to panic.

That's when she heard a noise in the corner of the mausoleum and realized she wasn't alone.

"Omigod!"

11. ELEVEN

"Who's in here?"

No one answered, but Maddie could distinctly hear the sound of something scraping against the floor along the far wall of the mausoleum.

"Rose?"

"Be careful, Maddie Graves." Rose's voice was barely a whisper. "Death is here."

Maddie swallowed hard, trying to tamp down the panic as it invaded her soul. "What does that mean?"

"I'm not the only presence that stayed behind," Rose said. "There's something else. There's something worse."

"And it's here now?"

"It's here and it's coming for you."

"Crap," Maddie muttered, extending her hands and moving toward the area where she believed she would find the door. "Nicky!"

"I STILL THINK you should describe what Maddie looks like naked for me," Brian said. "You did beat me up because I wanted to ask her out when we were in high school."

Nick scorched him with a look. "You do not want to go there."

"Come on," Brian pleaded. "She's stinking hot, man. She looks like she could be a model. I mean ... did you see her legs in that dress last night?"

"I see her legs every night."

"Now you're just rubbing it in."

"Brian, the only reason I'm not beating you up again is because there are too many witnesses," Nick warned. "Stop talking about Maddie being naked."

"Just for clarification, I don't think he's asking to see Maddie naked," Aaron said.

Max raised his hand. "I am."

Aaron wagged a finger in his face. "Don't make things worse," he said. "I think Brian just wants you to describe what you get to cuddle up next to every night. You don't have to go into great detail ... ."

"Yes, he does," Max said.

"Seriously, you're not helping us here," Aaron said. "Just ... give us a hint, man. How great is her body?"

Nick knew that smiling was akin to encouraging them, but every time he thought of Maddie naked he couldn't help but grin. When he realized what he as doing, he forced a frown onto his face. "You guys make me sick. You're talking about the woman I love like she's a piece of meat."

"Oh, you're such a goner," Aaron said. "Why don't you just propose now and get it over with?"

"Because we want to live together and have fun dating first," Nick said. "Don't worry, we're going to get married. It's not a matter of if. It's a matter of when, and the when is ... ." Nick broke off when he heard the whisper. He thought he was imagining it at first. He thought the words were nothing but a trick of his imagination on the wind. Three months before he would've ignored the prickling on the back of his neck. He would've ignored the whisper.

That was before Olivia's ghost manifested enough power to propel Nick to Maddie in time to save her life, though. That was before Olivia's ghost tipped him off that Maddie was being stalked in her own home.

Nick snapped his head up, scanning the cemetery. "Where's Maddie?"

Brian, Max, and Aaron didn't pick up on the change in Nick's demeanor.

"Just tell us if she's a real blonde," Max suggested.

"Where is Maddie?" Nick repeated, moving away from the men and desperately searching the cemetery with his busy brown eyes. After a few moments, his gaze fell on Christy and he exhaled a heavy sigh of relief. The boisterous redhead wouldn't leave Maddie. He was sure of that. When Nick realized Christy was alone, though, his heart plummeted. He ignored the spewed questions from his friends and broke into a run as he raced toward Christy.

Maddie was in trouble. Olivia was warning him of something. He just didn't know what.

"I DON'T KNOW what's in the corner over there but I'm officially terrified," Maddie said, her hands finding the heavy metal of the door. She almost cried out in relief. The scuffling sounds from the other side of the mausoleum were getting closer. Maddie had no idea what was stalking her in the dark. She knew it couldn't be good, though. "Come on."

She fumbled along until she found the doorknob and wrapped her hand around it, frantically tugging as she desperately tried to find literal light so she could chase away the dark. She had to get out of here.

"Nick is coming."

Olivia's voice soothed Maddie even though she couldn't see her in the murky dark. "Mommy?"

"It's okay, Maddie," Olivia said. "He's coming. I warned him."

"There's something in here," Maddie said. "There's something ... horrible ... in here."

"I know," Olivia said.

"The door is locked. I can't get it open."

"Take a breath, Maddie," Olivia instructed. "You're going to pass out if you're not careful."

"What's in here? I can't see it. I can hear it. It's getting closer."

"I don't know what it is," Olivia said. "Something evil has manifested here."

"Can it hurt me?"

"I ... I don't know, Maddie. Just try to relax. Nick will be here any second."

"What if he's too late?"

"He'll never be too late," Olivia said. "You're destined for happily ever after together. He won't be late. Trust him."

"WHERE IS MADDIE?" Nick snapped as he approached Christy.

The redhead, who was busy watching squirrels frolic in the nearby tree, seemed surprised at Nick's vehemence. "She's right over ... ." Christy frowned. "She was right there."

"Where?"

"She was by the mausoleum," Christy said.

Nick pushed past her and increased his pace, beating a straight path toward the mausoleum. Aaron stopped at Christy's side, confused and concerned. "I have no idea what's going on," he said. "He was in the middle of saying something to us and then it was like ... I don't know ... he heard a voice or something. Then he started screaming about Maddie."

Christy didn't like the sound of that. "Look in the mausoleum," she ordered.

Nick reached the door and tugged on the handle, frustrated when it refused to open. "Maddie?" There was no answer from inside so Nick pounded on the door mercilessly. "Maddie?"

"What's going on?" Marla asked, appearing from the other side of the mausoleum.

Christy narrowed her eyes suspiciously. "Where were you?"

"Looking around," Marla said, making a face. Cassidy appeared on her heels. Her face was hard to read, but Christy was sure she saw guilt reflected there.

"Have you seen Maddie?" Christy asked.

"Maddie?" Nick pounded on the mausoleum door again.

"I'm sure she's not in there," Marla said. "Maybe she went back to the house."

"She wouldn't have left without telling me," Nick seethed. "There's nowhere else she could be."

"There's no reason to freak out," Marla said. "I'm sure your precious Maddie is perfectly fine. She's probably hiding because she knows it will get your motor running. Then, just when you're really panicked, she'll appear out of nowhere just so you can fawn all over you."

"If you don't shut your mouth, I'm going to shut it for you," Nick warned. He pounded on the mausoleum door again. "Maddie? Answer me!"

"Dude, let me help you," Aaron said, using his hips to edge Nick out of the way. "This door sticks. There's a trick to opening it. Hold on."

Aaron fiddled with the handle for a few moments and Nick's heart jumped to his throat when the door sprung open. He pushed Aaron out of the way and bolted into the room, his heart rolling painfully when he saw Maddie's crumpled form on the hard, cement floor.

"Maddie." He dropped to his knees and crawled to her carefully, terrified he would find her hurt – or worse – when he finally touched her. When his hands made contact with her shoulders, he rolled her so he could study her face.

Her eyes were closed and she almost looked as if she was sleeping. It was obvious she'd been crying, though. Something terrible had happened to her. "Love?" He slipped an arm under her waist as he fought to hold on to the tattered remnants of his resolve. When he cradled Maddie to his chest he was relieved to find she was still breathing. He'd breathed life back into her still lungs before. She was doing it for herself this time, though. That had to be a good sign, right?

"Should we call an ambulance?" Aaron asked, his face a mask of worry and fright.

Nick hoisted Maddie up into his arms and stood, moving out of the mausoleum and into the sunlight. A hint of movement caught his attention, and when Maddie's chin moved a second time, a raw sob escaped his throat. "Maddie?"

"Nicky," she murmured.

"I've got you," Nick said, clutching her tightly as he started walking back toward Aaron's house. "I've got you."

"IS SHE OKAY?" Christy asked, letting herself into the library and closing the door behind her.

Maddie regained consciousness before they reached the house, although she was confused and incoherent. Instead of questioning her in front of everyone, Nick told the others to find something to do while he took care of her. He didn't want her to blurt anything out in front of an audience.

For the past five minutes he'd been rubbing her shoulders and trying to get her to drink a bottle of water while she regained her senses. He was still waiting to question her.

"The color is coming back to her cheeks," Nick said, brushing his thumb against her lip. "She still seems a little out of it."

"I am so sorry," Christy said. "She saw the ghost from last night, and she wanted me to act as a lookout while she talked to her. I honestly didn't see the harm in it. I wasn't paying close enough attention, though. This is my fault."

"It's my fault," Nick said. "I should've stayed with her."

"It's no one's fault," Maddie said, finally speaking. "Don't talk about me like I'm not even here."

Nick exhaled heavily. "Are you okay, Mad? Do you want me to take you to the hospital?"

"I'm fine," Maddie said, lifting her hand. It was shaking, and Nick clasped it with his own and lowered his eyes until they met hers.

"You don't look fine, love."

"She actually looks better than you," Christy said. "You're as white as a ghost."

"Ha, ha."

"I wasn't joking," Christy said. She reached over and patted Maddie's hand reassuringly. "What happened?"

"I'm not a hundred percent sure," Maddie said, leaning forward as Nick eased himself into a sitting position beside her and snaked his arm around her waist. "I was talking to Rose ... ."

"Who is Rose?"

"She's Aaron's dead grandmother."

"I ... okay," Nick said. "We'll talk about that later ... when we're alone upstairs." Or at home, he added silently. "Why did you shut the door?"

"I didn't shut the door," Maddie said. "I left it propped open. I needed the light. I just wanted to talk to Rose when I could be assured I didn't have an audience."

"How long were you in there?"

"Not long," Maddie said. "She told me who she was. She was kind of sad and I was trying to get her to open up about what happened to her. She finally admitted she was murdered and then ... well ... the door slammed shut."

Nick frowned. "That door opens from the outside," he said. "That means someone closed it from the outside. There was no wind. It couldn't have blown shut. It was too heavy."

"It wasn't me," Christy said.

"I didn't think it was you," Nick said. "You were watching the squirrels. The guys were over with me. Lauren wasn't with us but I never lost sight of her. That means it had to be either Marla or Cassidy who closed the door."

"It also means they probably knew Maddie was inside when they did it," Christy said. "I should've been paying closer attention. I'm so sorry. Did you pass out because you were scared?"

"I ... I'm not sure I passed out."

"What do you mean?" Nick asked.

"There was something in the mausoleum," Maddie said. "Rose warned me that she wasn't the only thing that stayed behind after death. The thing is, I could hear something physically moving."

She looked earnest, and she clearly believed what she was saying, but Nick had no idea what she was talking about. "I don't know what that means, Mad."

"I don't either," Maddie said. "I just know something was in that room with me. I tried to open the door, but it was like the handle was stuck."

"I know," Nick said, running his hand down the back of her head. "I couldn't get it open from outside either. Aaron had to do it for me."

"How did you know she was in trouble?" Christy asked. "Aaron said you were in the middle of a sentence and then you just took off because you knew something was wrong."

"Olivia came to me."

"She's done that a few times now, hasn't she?"

"She has," Nick said. "I knew I had to get to Maddie."

"She came to me, too," Maddie said. "She kept telling me to hold on. She told me you were coming. I called for you and then ... I don't know what happened. I felt something behind me. I felt a ... hand ... on my shoulder. The next thing I knew I was waking up in your arms."

"It's okay," Nick said, kissing her forehead and tightening his arms around her. "It's okay."

"I'm not sure it is," Christy said seriously. "We need to come up with a story to tell those people out there, and we need to do it fast."

"Do you think they're suspicious?" Maddie asked, worried.

"I think they passed suspicious when Nick started beating on the mausoleum door and having a complete and total meltdown while screaming your name," Christy said.

"This isn't good."

12. TWELVE

"You saw a raccoon?" Aaron's eyes widened incredulously. "You passed out because you saw a raccoon?"

"I'm so sorry," Maddie said, her back resting against Nick's chest as he snuggled up behind her. "I'm mortified."

"It's fine," Aaron said. "You scared us to death, but it's fine. I don't understand what happened, though."

"I was just looking around the mausoleum," Maddie explained. "It's really pretty in there, by the way. Although, you might want to have someone dust it from time to time. It's a little dirty... especially the floor."

"How did you get locked in?" Max asked.

"That's a pretty good question," Nick said, shifting his gaze to Marla and Cassidy, an unsaid accusation hanging in the air.

"Why are you looking at me?" Marla asked, nonplussed.

"Because that door closes from the outside," Nick said, not backing down. "Brian, Max, and Aaron were with me. Lauren was less than twenty feet away from me the whole time Maddie was gone. Christy was close, but not close enough to close the door. That leaves you and Cassidy as the only suspects."

Cassidy's face turned a mottled shade of red as Marla feigned total shock and disgust. "Are you actually accusing me of locking Maddie in that mausoleum?"

"Yes."

"Why would I possibly do that?"

"Because you're evil," Nick replied, not missing a beat. "I know it was you. Don't bother denying it." He shifted his gaze to Cassidy. "I expected better from you. I know you're angry with me, but do you really think a junior high school prank that almost resulted in Maddie being seriously hurt is the best way to deal with your issues?"

"I ... ."

"Don't accuse her of doing anything," Marla said. "You have no proof. Personally, I think Maddie locked herself in the mausoleum so she could get attention. That would be totally like her."

Nick opened his mouth, every hateful thought he had on the tip of his tongue and ready to be unleashed, but Aaron stilled him with a hand on his shoulder. "I believe Marla," he said.

Marla stilled, surprise washing over her features. "You do?"

"Of course I do," Aaron said. "Only a truly pathetic person would lock someone in the mausoleum."

"I ... um ... right," Marla said.

"The good news is that we can prove it wasn't Marla," Aaron said.

"We can?" Nick asked, glancing up at Aaron for a hint of what he was getting at.

"My mother was worried that grave robbers would try and steal from the mausoleum so she had cameras installed out there," Aaron said. "I can go up to the security room and look at the video feed. That will prove that Marla and Cassidy are innocent."

"I think we all should go and take a look," Christy said.

"Well, wait just a second ... ." Marla said, exchanging a worried look with Cassidy. "Is that really necessary?"

"I think it is," Brian said, catching on to the game. "If you and Cassidy didn't shut Maddie in the mausoleum, that means someone else did. There could be some sort of deviant hanging around the grounds. We all could be in danger. We can't have that. I wouldn't feel safe with a deviant on the grounds."

"I think this is an outstanding idea," Max said. "Plus, we have a police officer here. If we catch someone on the feed, Nick can arrest the guilty person."

"He's off duty," Marla said.

"That doesn't mean I can't arrest someone if they commit a crime," Nick said. "In this case, it would be my personal pleasure."

"Let's go up and look at the video," Aaron said. "After all that's handled, I don't know about anyone else, but I'm starving. How about you, Miss Maddie? Did the raccoon scare the hunger out of you?"

"I'm really sorry I worried everyone," Maddie said, clasping her hands together on her lap.

"Don't worry about," Aaron said, waving off her concerns. "We were getting complacent. We needed a little drama. Things were getting boring."

"I'm still sorry."

"It wouldn't have happened if someone didn't lock you in the mausoleum," Nick said. "Let's go take a look at the video feed. I can't wait to see who the culprit is."

"It was just supposed to be a joke," Cassidy blurted out, her face contorting as hot tears started spilling down her cheeks. "I swear. We didn't mean to hurt her. We just thought it would be funny to lock her in there with the dead bodies."

"Why?" Marla asked, gritting her teeth. "Why did you just say that?"

"They're going to see the video," Cassidy said. "They're going to know it was us."

"There is no video out there," Aaron said. "I was bluffing."

"I knew it," Marla grumbled.

"We also knew you were the one who locked Maddie inside," Max said.

"How could you possibly know that?"

"You're the only one pathetic enough to do it," Aaron said.

"You're also the only one mean enough to do it," Brian added. "Maddie has been nothing but sweet and nice since she got here. You've been the aggressive one."

"I'm so sorry," Cassidy said. "I just ... it was a horrible thing to do."

"It was a horrible thing to do," Nick said. "Maddie could've been seriously injured."

"Hey, it's not our fault Maddie scared herself silly with a raccoon," Marla said. "That's all on her."

"Marla, I've had enough of you," Aaron said. "I think you ... and your little friend ... should be going."

"What? You're kicking me out?"

"I am," Aaron said.

"Wait a second," Maddie said, leaning forward. "I'm not sure that's necessary."

"Maddie," Nick groaned. "Let him kick them out."

"I'm sure Marla and Cassidy are sorry," Maddie countered. "Maybe this will be an important lesson for both of them."

"Marla doesn't learn lessons," Christy said. "She's too stupid to learn lessons."

"Shut up, Christy," Marla snapped.

Aaron studied Maddie's serious face for a moment, trying to get a read on her. Finally, he turned back to Marla. "You can stay ... ."

Marla smiled triumphantly.

"If you apologize to Maddie and promise not to say one more snarky thing to her this entire weekend," Aaron said.

Marla made a face. "Excuse me?"

"That goes for both of you," Aaron said, glancing at Cassidy pointedly. "I don't know you very well, Cassidy, but you appear to be sorry for what you did. I'm hoping you're willing to apologize and put this behind you ... and I mean all of it. I think it's time you realized Nick and Maddie aren't your enemies. You're not hurting anyone but yourself by holding onto this grudge."

Cassidy bit her lower lip, conflicted. Finally, she squared her shoulders and met Maddie's curious gaze. "I really am sorry for what we did," she said. "I would never try to physically hurt you. It was mean ... and stupid ... and really juvenile. I won't do anything like it again."

"Thank you," Maddie said, her voice low.

Aaron turned to Marla expectantly.

"Fine," Marla said. "I'm sorry we locked you in the mausoleum. It was a joke. There. Are you happy?"

Aaron glanced at Maddie for confirmation.

"I'm not happy," Maddie said. "I am willing to let it go, though."

"Good," Aaron said, moving toward the door. "Can we put this unfortunate incident behind us and eat?"

Maddie wasn't sure her stomach was settled enough for food, but she was sure she wanted everyone to focus on something else besides her. "That sounds like a great idea."

"CAN'T you try to eat at least half of the sandwich?" Nick asked, tapping the side of Maddie's plate for emphasis. "You only took two bites."

After a few furtive glances – and open glares on Nick and Christy's part – everyone settled around the patio table for a leisurely lunch. Maddie tried to hide her lack of appetite by pushing the food around on her plate, but Nick wasn't about to be fooled.

"I'm trying," Maddie said, forcing a weak smile for his benefit. "My stomach is still a little iffy."

"I understand that, Mad," Nick said patiently. "I also think, if you force yourself to take a few bites, you're going to realize that you're hungrier than you realize."

"I agree with Nick," Christy said. "You've had a big morning. You should stockpile some fuel so we can have some more drama and fun after lunch. Maybe we can have an equally big afternoon."

"I love drama and fun," Lauren said, grinning.

Maddie picked up the tuna sandwich and made a big show of biting into it. Nick watched her as she chewed, refusing to turn away until she swallowed. "Are you happy?"

"Not until you eat half of the sandwich," Nick said, forking some potato salad into his mouth.

"He's like a mother hen," Max teased.

"He's my mother hen," Maddie countered, leaning over and kissing him on the cheek. "I promise I'm fine."

"I'm not going to believe you until half of that sandwich disappears into your mouth," Nick said. "That's the rule of the afternoon."

Maddie sighed. "Fine. You really are a mother hen, though."

"I'm your mother hen," Nick corrected, internally smiling when she picked the sandwich back up and started munching on it.

"So, after we all watch Maddie force her lunch down, what does everyone want to do?" Brian asked.

"I thought we were playing basketball," Max said.

"I'm sticking close to Maddie until I'm sure she's on solid ground," Nick said. "I promise to play basketball, but I want to give it a few hours."

"I guess that's understandable," Max grumbled.

"He can't play basketball until he catches me a turtle," Maddie said. "He promised me he would do it yesterday."

"What is it with you and turtles?" Christy asked.

Maddie shrugged. "I don't know. I've just always liked them."

"And you always catch them for her?" Christy asked, turning her attention to Nick.

"Yup. I'm the biggest and baddest turtle hunter in northern Lower Michigan."

"What do you do when you catch them?" Lauren asked.

"She pets them for five minutes, gives them names, and then releases them," Nick said. "It's a lot of hard work for very little reward."

"I always reward you," Maddie countered.

Nick tilted his head to the side, considering. "I guess you do," he conceded. "I can honestly say the rewards have gotten better over the past few weeks."

Maddie grinned, her strength returning after a few wayward hours. "I promise to reward you well if you catch me a big one."

"Well, I can't ignore that challenge now, can I?" Nick leaned over to give her a kiss, surprised to find the entire sandwich gone. "Did you eat that whole thing?"

"I guess I was hungrier than I thought," Maddie admitted sheepishly.

"Score one for the mother hen," Nick said, extending his hand. "Come on, my Maddie. If you're lucky, I might catch you two turtles today."

"I'm feeling pretty lucky these days."

"We both are," Nick said.

13. THIRTEEN

"The river is fast moving today," Maddie said, pulling her blonde hair on top of her head and securing it in place so she wouldn't risk getting it wet or dirty. "We must have gotten more rain than I realized last night."

Nick glanced at her, smiling at her lovely face in all of its simplistic glory. She wasn't the type of woman who wore a lot of makeup, but on the days her face was bare and free, she was absolutely exquisite. And, while he preferred her hair loose so he could run his fingers through it, there was something appealing about the way she carried herself when the flaxen waves were corralled.

They'd changed to simple shorts and shirts, Maddie opting for a black tank top that showed off her sculpted shoulders. Maddie was one of those women who gave a hundred percent to everything, and that included working out. When they ran together, Nick often found he had to pace himself if he didn't want to fall behind. Her body was lithe and strong – and it was all his.

"Where is your mind?" Maddie asked, placing her hands on her narrow hips and shooting him a curious look.

"Where is my mind all of the time?" Nick asked, refusing to be embarrassed. "I was thinking how cute you looked in your little outfit."

Maddie glanced down, making a face. "Sometimes I think you just say things to see if you can charm me."

"Sometimes I do."

"Was this one of those times?"

"No," Nick said. "I was honestly thinking how much I love the way you look when you're dressed down. I love it when you get dressed up, don't get me wrong. But when you're like this – when you're obviously comfortable – I think that might be when I love you best."

"Wow," Maddie said. "I should get attacked by a ... raccoon ... every day if this is the way you're going to treat me." She was going for levity, but her words caused Nick to sober. "I shouldn't have said that. I'm such an idiot."

"It's okay, Mad," Nick said, looking over his shoulder to make sure no one was within hearing distance. The rest of their party was still sitting on the patio, and while Nick and Maddie were a point of interest, no one could hear what they were talking about above the rush of the river. "You just scared me. Olivia only comes to me when you're in real trouble."

"Do you know what's funny? She's come to you three different times now. I think that's a commentary on me and the fact that I just can't quite seem to stay out of trouble."

"I don't think that's funny," Nick said. "I just got you. I'm not ready to lose you."

"I promise you won't lose me."

"We both know you can't make that promise," Nick said. "You can promise not to leave me – which is one promise I'm holding you to forever – and you can promise me that you'll be careful. You can't promise that someone ... or something, for that matter ... won't try to take you from me."

"Actually, I can promise you that you won't lose me," Maddie sad. "Mom told me that some things are destiny, including our happily ever after. I believe with my whole heart that we'll get it."

"I think we've already gotten it, Mad," Nick said, kissing the tip of her nose.

"Not until I get a turtle."

Nick sighed. "You're a demanding turtle wrangler," he said. "Let's find one. I'm afraid that if I don't catch one your male fan club on the patio is going to get bored and try to charm you by showing me up."

"Oh, no one could ever show you up," Maddie said.

"That won't stop them from trying."

"Well, in that case ... ." She held out her hand expectantly. Nick knew what was cupped in her palm and he took it wordlessly, rubbing his fingers over the smooth surface of the Petoskey stone. This was a little ritual of hers, and it was one he never grew tired of. Maddie pressed her lips to his softly. "For luck."

"OKAY, does anyone else think those two act like they've stepped off the pages of a bodice ripper and only agreed to join the mortals for a weekend because they were bored?" Lauren asked, smiling as she watched Nick and Maddie splash around in the water.

"They're definitely living in a fantasy world I've never been to," Brian said. "They're so happy."

"I love them together," Christy said, grabbing a bottle of water from the drink cart and settling on one of the lounge chairs. "They give me hope."

"That you'll be jealous of them forever?" Aaron teased.

"That there's someone out there for everyone," Christy said. "Look how long they pined for each other. Their happiness is proof that neither one of them was ever going to be content with someone else.

"I've always believed there's one person out there for everyone," she continued. "I can feel you guys rolling your eyes over there ... stop it. Those two prove I was right."

"Well, I think it's definitely true for them," Brian said. "Their hearts joined a long time ago. No one else ever had a shot."

"Then maybe Nick shouldn't have been dating around and crushing women while he was waiting for Maddie to come back to him," Marla suggested.

"I thought you were going to let this go," Aaron said.

"Why should I let it go? Nick crushed one of my very best friends in the world." Marla patted Cassidy's hand. "This is just torture for the poor girl."

"Then why did you bring her?" Max asked.

"Excuse me? I thought she deserved a fun weekend."

"That's not why you brought her," Lauren said, shooting a sympathetic look in Cassidy's direction. The woman was fixated on Maddie and Nick, and with each shared touch and giggle, Lauren could see the misery weighing Cassidy down. "You brought her to upset Maddie."

"I did not," Marla protested.

Lauren ignored Marla and focused on Cassidy. "Listen, I don't know you very well, Cassidy, but I think you're selling yourself short," she said. "You seem like a nice woman caught in a bad situation. I get that you thought you had a future with Nick, but I also think you realize that he didn't feel the same way about you."

"You were at a disadvantage," Christy said. "You had only been in town a few years when you and Nick started dating. You'd heard about his six-month cycle, and you'd even heard about Maddie, but without ever being able to see them together you never realized just how attached to one another they were."

"See, we all went to school together," Lauren said. "When we were in elementary school, everyone thought Maddie and Nick were weird because that was when boys and girls weren't supposed to like each other. Those two were always together, though."

"Then, when we hit middle school, Maddie went through an awkward phase," she continued. "We all did, but Maddie's was kind of harsh."

"She looked like a walking pimple," Marla said, smirking.

"You should talk, pit stain," Lauren said. "Your hair was always greasy, you were flat as a board, and you didn't need a bra until right before you graduated. You started stuffing in seventh grade, but everyone knew because they could see the lumps from the tissue paper."

"You shut up," Marla ordered.

"No, you shut up," Lauren shot back.

"Yes, Marla, please shut up," Aaron said. "Lauren and Christy are trying to help Cassidy. I know that messes with your master plan, but shut up and let them try to help."

Marla wrinkled her nose, crossing her arms over her chest as she glared at Aaron with unveiled contempt. "I don't think I like the way you're talking to me."

"Then leave," Aaron suggested.

"By the time high school hit, Maddie and Nick were ... set," Lauren said. "We all knew there was something different about their relationship. The funny thing is, none of us ever doubted they would end up together."

"Speak for yourself," Brian said. "I had big dreams of stealing her away from Nick."

"You never had a chance with me in the game," Max said.

"Oh, please, none of you had a chance with Nick in the game," Christy said. "As far as anyone was concerned, those two were the only ones on their particular team."

"If all of that is true, why didn't they get together as teenagers?" Cassidy asked. "Why did Maddie run away from Nick and abandon him? Marla says she only came back because she couldn't hack it in the real world. She ran back home to what was safe. What's to stop her from taking off again?"

"Marla is filling your head with crap," Christy said, fighting to tamp down her irritation. "What Marla isn't telling you is that she had a huge crush on Nick in high school."

"What?" Cassidy was surprised ... and puzzled. Marla had never mentioned anything of the sort.

"That's not true," Marla said hurriedly.

"It is true," Lauren said. "She was infatuated with Nick in high school. If she's telling you otherwise, she's lying."

"I don't understand," Cassidy said, legitimately confused.

"Marla cozied up to you after you started dating Nick," Christy said. "You should know that after Maddie left town Marla tried every trick in the book to get him to date her. He refused. He was never interested in her."

"You shut your filthy mouth," Marla snapped.

"Nick was the ultimate prize for Marla," Lauren said. "He was just a prize she could never lay claim to. It made her bitter. I'm guessing she became friends with you just so she could have a reason to be close to Nick."

"Never think, not even for a second, that Marla wouldn't have tried to steal Nick from you if the opportunity arose," Christy said.

Cassidy swiveled, fixing Marla with a hard look. "Is that true? Did you just befriend me because I was dating Nick?"

"Don't listen to them," Marla said. "They've always been jealous of me."

"What reason would we have to lie?" Christy asked, opting for logic. "Other than being happy for Maddie and Nick, we don't have a dog in this fight. Have you ever asked yourself why Marla does?"

Cassidy rubbed the back of her neck as she chewed on her lip. Christy was convinced at least some of the wisdom they'd been imparting on her was starting to sink in. From the look on Marla's face, she was worrying about the same thing.

"They're messing with your mind," Marla hissed.

"Shut up, Marla," Max said. "Everyone is sick of hearing you talk. Give Cassidy a chance to think for herself. I know that's not what you want because you've been thinking for her, but leave her alone for a minute. Good grief, you're just such a ... pain in the ass."

"I can't believe I slept with you," Marla said, her eyes narrow slits.

"Me either," Max said. "It would've been so much better if you could've just shut your mouth when we were done."

Cassidy turned back out to the river, watching as Maddie handed Nick something.

"What is she giving him?" Lauren asked. "It looks like a rock."

"It's a Petoskey stone," Christy said. "He catches turtles for her and she gives him Petoskey stones for luck. They've been doing it since they were kids."

"What does he do with the stones?" Aaron asked.

"He keeps them," Cassidy said, deflating as a memory washed over her. "He has a whole box of them in his house. I found them when we were dating. He only ever let me go over there a few times, and I was going through his stuff one day because I was curious, and I found them. I thought he collected them for himself, but when I gave him one he thanked me for it and left it on his back deck. He didn't even look at it again."

"Oh," Christy said, pity for Cassidy welling in her chest. "I'm sure that … ."

"Don't," Cassidy said, things finally slipping into place for her. "He kept the stones because they were all he had of her. They were a tie to her. He never wanted a tie to me. I know that. It's just … ."

"It hurts," Christy supplied. "I get that."

"I loved him," Cassidy said. "I thought we were in love. I thought we were building a future. It turns out, though, that she was the only future he ever wanted."

"It's better that you know now," Lauren said. "Nothing was ever going to keep Nick and Maddie apart. Not in the grand scheme of things, at least. Let's say you did manage to hold onto him longer than the original six months … he still wasn't ever going to love you like you deserve."

"I know," Cassidy said, fighting off tears as Maddie squealed and Nick twirled her around while she watched the interplay with a growing sense of dread and disgust – both of which were aimed inward. "I have to let this go."

"You do," Christy agreed. "The sooner you let this go, the sooner you'll realize that you're free to find someone of your own to love."

"It will never be Nick Winters, though," Cassidy said.

"No."

"You don't know that," Marla said. "You … ."

"Shut up, Marla." Everyone said the words at the same time, including Cassidy, and Marla was taken aback. "What the … ?"

"I'll pay you a thousand dollars if you're quiet for an hour," Aaron offered. "I'll up it to five grand if you keep your mouth shut the entire evening."

Christy giggled. "I would take it if I were you. That's the best offer you're going to get."

14. FOURTEEN

"Will you stop fidgeting?" Christy pulled the eyeliner pencil away from Maddie's face and waited.

"I'm sorry," Maddie said. "It's just that trusting someone else to put something that close to my eye makes me nervous."

The two women were in Maddie and Nick's room getting ready for dinner, and because she liked to doll people up, Christy insisted on doing Maddie's makeup and hair. Nick, dressed in khakis and a button-down shirt, wandered out of the bathroom and smiled as he watched Maddie try to wrestle Christy's hand away from her face.

"I'm not going to poke you in the eye," Christy said. "Don't you trust me?"

"Of course I trust you."

"Then hold still," Christy said. She held Maddie's chin with one hand and swooped the liner over her eyelid quickly, duplicating the effort on the other eye a few moments later. She stood back to admire her handiwork and then started rummaging around in the makeup bag until she found the tube of mascara she was looking for. "One more thing."

"Oh, come on, I don't need that much makeup."

"It's not about needing it," Christy said. "It's about making your-self look hot for Nick."

"Don't bring me into this," Nick said. "I think she's beautiful no matter what."

"No one asked you," Christy said, rolling her eyes. "This is a woman thing."

"Well, my woman doesn't seem to think she needs it," Nick pointed out.

"Just ... sit there and look pretty," Christy instructed, rolling her eyes until they landed back on Maddie. "Hold still."

Five minutes later Christy was happy with her masterpiece and she left Maddie and Nick so she could dress herself before heading downstairs. Nick watched Maddie study her reflection in the mirror, curious what she was thinking. *What does she see when she looks at herself?*

"I think it's too much," Maddie said, leaning forward and widening her eyes. "I look like a raccoon."

Nick smirked. "I think we've had enough raccoons for one night," he said. "If it's any consolation, I think you look ... amazing."

"You always say that," Maddie said, swiveling in the chair and standing up so Nick could take in the full package. The black sheath was loose and yet it left little to the imagination as it fell to the middle of her thigh. The spaghetti straps of the dress set off the bronze hue of her skin, and the baby pink camisole underneath the dress was giving Nick ideas – most of which revolved around finding out if her underwear matched.

"You look beautiful, my Maddie."

Maddie tucked a strand of her blonde hair behind her ear, smiling ruefully as she tilted her head to the side. Her adorable mannerisms, including the head tilt, often tugged at Nick's heart in surprising ways.

"You always know exactly what to say," Maddie said.

"You always know exactly how to make me feel so I know what to say."

Maddie slipped into his arms, resting her head against his chest as he swayed slightly. Sitting through dinner with a group of people was slipping down in importance on his evening to-do list.

"It's too bad we're not in a real hotel," he said. "If we were, we could order room service and eat in bed."

"That would kind of defeat the purpose of me sitting through that torturous makeup session with Christy, wouldn't it?"

Nick pursed his lips as he brought his hands up and cupped Maddie's chin. "You do look beautiful, love. I'm excited to show you off to everyone."

"How about we eat dinner, have one drink after, and then make some excuses about having to go to bed early? We can use my experience with the raccoon this afternoon as an easy out."

"That sounds absolutely perfect to me."

"WOW!" Max's mouth dropped open when he saw Maddie walk into the library.

"Double wow," Aaron said. "You look hot, Maddie. How come you didn't dress that way in high school?"

Maddie's cheeks burned under the praise. "Um ... ."

"She was too shy," Christy said. "She wouldn't have dressed this way for dinner tonight if it wasn't for me. I'm thinking of dressing her every day for the rest of her life. She's like a human Barbie doll. I just can't help myself."

"Huh," Brian said, cocking his head to look at Maddie from a different angle. "Now that you mention it, she does look exactly like a Barbie doll."

"I do not," Maddie said, glancing at Nick for help.

"You kind of do look like a Barbie doll," Nick said, his expression rueful. "As long as no one confuses me with Ken, though, I'm not complaining." He kissed her cheek and then moved over to the drink cart. "Do you want a glass of wine, Mad?"

"Sure."

Christy patted the spot on the leather sofa next to her and Maddie obediently sat down. When she scanned the room, she couldn't help but notice that Cassidy and Marla were suspiciously absent. "Where are ... ?"

"The terrible twosome?" Aaron asked, cutting her off.

Maddie nodded.

"They had a bit of a ... fight ... this afternoon," Lauren said. "As a distraction, Marla decided to take Cassidy to the fair in town. I'm kind of hoping Marla finds someone else to pique her interest so she doesn't come back."

"What did they fight about?"

"Oh ... um ... ." Christy bit her bottom lip.

"We explained a few things to Cassidy this afternoon," Lauren said, unruffled.

"Uh-oh," Maddie said. "I'm not going to like this, am I?"

"I have no idea," Lauren said. "The simple truth is that Cassidy has been operating in the dark regarding Marla's motivations. We set her straight on a few things."

"I'm almost afraid to ask," Nick said.

"We just explained that you and Maddie were always destined to be together," Aaron said.

"We also explained that Marla has always had a thing for Nick," Christy said. "Cassidy had a right to know that Marla would've stolen Nick from her in a heartbeat."

"Okay, you need to stop saying things like that," Nick said. "The thought of touching Marla ... ugh." He involuntarily shuddered.

Maddie smirked. "Oh, I don't know," she said. "I think you guys would've made a cute couple."

"Are you trying to give me an aneurism?"

"I'm just teasing you," Maddie said. "If you would've dated Marla I would've felt the Earth tilt on its axis and run back up here sooner so I could kill her."

Nick wrinkled his nose. "Wow. If I knew that, I would've gone out with her just to get you back home."

"I don't know," Maddie said. "I think things worked out like they were supposed to. I shouldn't have left, but I'm not sorry I came back when I did. I can't imagine being any happier than this."

"You and me both, love."

"Okay, I'm going to puke," Max said, putting his empty glass down on the coffee table. "We need to have something to eat if I'm going to have something to regurgitate."

"Well, thank you for that visual," Aaron deadpanned.

"Hey, blame the sappy twosome here," Max said. "They're sweet enough to give me a cavity ... and a stomachache."

"Don't listen to him, Mad," Nick said. "You're just sweet enough to be perfect."

"Ugh," everyone said in unison.

Nick grinned at his blonde. "Is it wrong that I'm starting to get off on grossing everyone out?"

Maddie shook her head while everyone else voiced their own opinion. "Yes!"

I THINK I had a little too much to drink," Maddie admitted, listing to the side and grabbing the bedpost to keep from stumbling.

"I know," Nick said, lifting his eyebrows and smiling. "You had three whole glasses. I think you're turning into a lush."

Maddie's face flushed, partially from the wine and partially because she was embarrassed. "I'm sorry."

"Why?"

"Because ... well ... I'm drunk."

"You're not drunk, love," Nick said, tugging his shirt over his head and dropping it on the floor. "You're tipsy. Three glasses of wine doesn't a drunk make, even when someone isn't used to drinking. You'll be fine. Trust me."

Maddie giggled, her inhibitions nothing but a distant memory. "You look pretty with your shirt off."

Nick cocked an eyebrow. "Pretty?"

"You're very pretty," Maddie said, sidling up to him and running her hand down his chiseled chest. "You're beautiful."

"All right, maybe you are a little drunk," Nick conceded. "You don't feel sick to your stomach, do you?"

"Nope."

"Is your head spinning?"

"No more than usual when you take your shirt off."

Nick couldn't help but smile. She was adorable when she was bubbly. "So, love, what do you want to do?"

Maddie plopped down on the bed and gazed up at him mischievously. "I thought you could try to get to second base."

"Oh, honey, I have my eyes on a home run tonight," Nick said, pressing his lips to hers. "Maybe two of them."

"HOW DID you know this was here?" Cassidy asked, realizing she was a little tipsy as she bumped into a wall in the dark.

"All big mansions have secret passageways," Marla said, wrinkling her nose as she glanced around the dusty and dim hallway. "I saw Max going through a door I didn't even know was there last night. I've been dying to check it out."

"Where do you think these passages go?" Cassidy asked.

"I have no idea," Marla said. "Let's look around, though. This is kind of fun. It's like being in an episode of *Scooby Doo*."

"But ... we weren't invited to wander around this part of the house," Cassidy said. After three hours of drinking and talking, Marla convinced her that Christy and Lauren were merely trying to cause problems. Deep down, Cassidy realized Marla was a predator. Right now, though, she didn't have a lot of people to rely on. She'd decided that hanging out with the shark was better than hanging out alone. "What if Aaron finds out and gets mad?"

"Oh, who cares?" Marla asked, brushing of Cassidy's concerns. "The only reason he's being that way is because he wants to get into Christy's pants. He knows he won't be able to if he's mean to Maddie. Trust me. He doesn't like Maddie any more than we do."

Cassidy followed Marla down the hallway, fingering her gold cross pendant idly as she considered her friend's statement. "I'm starting to think that maybe Maddie isn't the problem," she admitted.

"Oh, good grief. Not you, too."

"I'm serious," Cassidy said. "Don't get me wrong, I still feel like she was underhanded in the way she went after Nick, but the truth is, I knew he didn't love me. I kept telling myself that if I could just hold on long enough he would wake up one day and realize that I was the one for him."

"That could still happen," Marla said. "Maddie and Nick aren't built to make it for the long haul. Nick only wanted Maddie because he raised her up in his head for ten years. She was like the white whale and he just had to have her. Now that he has her, he's going to play with her a little bit, and then he's going to realize she's not that great and dump her. You just have to wait for a few months."

"Do you really think so?" Cassidy didn't believe the statement, but her heart flopped anyway. *Could that possibly be true?* If she just sat back and let Nick and Maddie's relationship run its course, would she and Nick have another chance at love?

"I do think so," Marla said. "I ... holy crap. Look."

Cassidy snapped her head to the side and followed the sound of Marla's voice. The lighting in the hallway was dim, the only illumination coming from emergency lights at the top of the various corners and walls. When she rounded the corner, she found Marla standing in front of a huge window. Only ... it wasn't a window.

"Where are we?" Cassidy asked, keeping her voice low as her eyes fell on Nick and Maddie. They were rolling around on their bed, both in varying stages of undress, and they didn't look as if they had a care in the world – other than each other.

"I think we're looking through the other side of their mirror," Marla said, her gaze trained on Nick's chest as Maddie rubbed her hands up and down it. "Wow. I knew he probably looked good shirtless, but that is just ... ."

"What did you say?" Cassidy asked, mortified that she couldn't drag her eyes away from the tableau playing out in front of her. This was a private moment. No, this was *the* most private moment any couple could engage in. She shouldn't be watching this, and yet she couldn't make herself stop either.

"Nothing," Marla said, licking her lips. "You don't think they can hear us, do you?"

"I think, if they could, they would stop doing ... that. Wow. How often do you think she works out?"

Nick was dragging the spaghetti strap of Maddie's dress down as he moved his mouth to her neck. Marla and Cassidy could hear each gasp and soft kiss from where they were standing and yet it seemed as if Nick and Maddie were oblivious to the fact that they had an audience.

"This is wrong," Cassidy said finally, fighting back the sob trying to wrench itself from her throat. Nick had never looked at her the way he looked at Maddie. While their lovemaking had been good, even hot sometimes, it was never like this. Nick never went out of his way to touch her like he was doing with Maddie. It was as if Maddie was his oxygen and he would die if he couldn't run his fingertips over her skin.

That's when the final nail in the realization coffin slipped into place for Cassidy. No matter what she told herself – not matter how hard Marla tried to convince her otherwise – Nick Winters was in love with Maddie Graves. It wasn't infatuation. It wasn't a momentary lapse in judgment that he would think better of in a few weeks. It wasn't a temporary coupling that he was going to get bored with.

This was forever.

"She has to have had some work done," Marla said, tilting her head to the side. "No one has a body like that without surgery."

Cassidy shot her a dark look. "We're done here."

"Speak for yourself," Marla said. "I want to see if Nick has stamina. I'm betting Maddie just lays there and lets him do all the work."

It didn't look that way to Cassidy. "We're going," she said, grabbing Marla's arm. "They deserve some privacy."

"They don't deserve anything," Marla said, although she reluctantly followed the insistent woman and started moving back down the passageway. "Don't worry. It won't be long until you have him back."

"He's never coming back to me," Cassidy said, casting one more look over her shoulder when she heard Nick speak.

"I love you, my Maddie," he said, cupping her chin and staring soulfully into her eyes.

The sentiment and naked raw emotion in his eyes caused something inside of Cassidy to break. "He belongs with her," she said. "I get that now."

15. FIFTEEN

"Well, well, well. It looks like someone had a nice night."

Aaron's eyes were bloodshot, itchy reminders of the previous evening's shenanigans. Even though it was obvious he had a raging hangover he was jovial when he caught sight of Nick and Maddie walking into the dining room the next morning.

"It looks like you had a late night," Nick said, his fingers linked with Maddie's. "How late were you guys up?"

"Too late," Lauren grumbled, holding her head in her hands as she studied the pitcher of water in front of her. "I have horrible cottonmouth, and yet I'm too tired to pour my own glass of water. How sad is that?"

"How much did you guys drink?" Maddie asked, sinking into the open seat next to Christy and fixing her friend with a sympathetic look.

"Too much," Christy moaned.

"You smell like you're still drunk."

"It's seeping out of my pores," Christy said. "These ... idiots ... started mixing everything on the bar. I can't even tell you how much my head hurts."

Max slid the bottle of aspirin down the table in Christy's direction. "Medicate up, sport."

"Shut up, tool."

Nick smirked. He was officially glad he and Maddie retired early – and not just because their evening activities were the stuff of ever-lasting dreams. Now they could enjoy their afternoon while everyone else grumbled and napped. "See, you guys called us goody-goodies last night, but who is happier?"

"Oh, please," Brian said. "You two are happy because you were playing hide the salami upstairs all night. You're not fooling anyone. You're both all ... sparkly. If I wasn't already nauseated because of the quarts of vodka I drank last night, I would want to puke because you two are so sickly sweet."

"You're just jealous," Nick said, pouring juice into Maddie's cup as she doled eggs onto both of their plates. "We were good while you were bad and the universe rewarded us."

"The universe didn't reward you," Christy countered. "The universe punished us."

"You should drink some water," Maddie said. "You should probably try to have something with sugar in it, too. The juice will probably suffice. I've read that a lot of hangovers are exacerbated because alcohol leeches sugar from your body."

"You read that?"

"Yes."

"You make me want to punch you sometimes," Christy said, although Maddie had to smile when she reached for the juice.

"So, what is everyone going to do today?" Nick asked, winking at Maddie. "I was thinking we could play some really loud music and have that game of two-on-two Max has been begging for."

"I hate you," Max said. "Now you want to play basketball?"

"He only wants to play now because he knows he could beat all three of us with one hand tied behind his back," Brian said. "I'm onto his game."

"That shows what you know," Nick said. "I don't even want to play basketball. I just want to torture you guys. It's kind of fun. Do you want me to tell you how much I love Maddie again?"

"Oh, please, anything but that," Marla said, breezing into the room. Unlike the rest of Aaron's guests, she looked fresh and relaxed.

"When did you get back?" Aaron asked.

"Around ten."

"How come you didn't come in and party with us?"

"Because you were all sloppy drunk and I didn't want to be around annoying people," Marla said. "I went up to bed early. After looking at you guys, it's clear I made the right decision."

"There's a first time for everything," Lauren said.

"You look like you've been run over by a truck," Marla shot back.

"You look like my ass," Lauren replied.

"At least I don't smell like one."

Maddie pursed her lips, worried the breakfast was going to devolve into something truly horrifying if she didn't do something to stop it. "Where is Cassidy?"

Marla shrugged. "She's probably still in bed. She was ... weird last night."

"That's because we told her what your true intentions were," Christy said.

"Oh, don't worry, I set her straight about that," Marla said. "She knows you were just trying to drive a wedge between us. We're back to being BFFs."

"Then she's dumber than she looks," Max said.

"You're a pig," Marla said.

"Oink."

Nick pinched the bridge of his nose to ward off the oncoming headache. "I think I'm going to take Maddie to town this afternoon," he announced.

"Why?" Aaron asked.

"Well, for starters, you all are nursing some terrific hangovers and I don't want to be around for all the grousing," Nick said. "I also want to check on a few things in town."

Maddie remembered their plan to stop in at the house to make sure Maude didn't sneak back in while they were gone. "I think that's a good idea."

"We'll be back in time for dinner," Nick said.

"I'm probably going to sleep most of the day," Max admitted.

"I'm going to mainline aspirin and water and swear to never drink again," Lauren said.

"I'm going to take a bath and then a nap," Christy said.

"I'm going to do all of that," Aaron said.

The sound of someone clearing their throat caused everyone to shift their attention to the doorframe at the far end of the room where a timid looking maid was shuffling back and forth.

"What's up, Miranda?" Aaron asked.

"I hate to bother you, sir," Miranda said. "It's just ... we were cleaning the rooms, and we noticed that the young lady in the south wing isn't down here and she's not up in her room. Do you think it's okay for us to clean?"

"I guess," Aaron said, shrugging. "Do you know where Cassidy is?"

"I have no idea, sir," Miranda said. "It doesn't look like she slept in the bed, though. It's still made up."

Nick glanced at Marla. "You two came back together, right?"

Marla nodded.

"When was the last time you saw her?"

"Oh, um, up in the hallway right before bed," Marla said. "We talked for a little bit when we got back and then we separated."

"Did you actually see her go into the bedroom?"

"No. It was right around the corner, though. Where would she go?"

Nick turned his attention back to Miranda. "Are you sure she just didn't make the bed up herself?"

"I'm sure, sir."

Nick pursed his lips, shifting his eyes to Maddie momentarily before making a decision. "Take me up to her room."

"What do you think is going on?" Aaron asked, his eyes suddenly brighter. "Do you think she's really missing?"

"Probably not," Nick said. "She might just be walking around outside or something. It just seems weird to me that she didn't sleep in her bed last night. This isn't her house. Cassidy isn't generally the type of person who would wander around someone else's property by herself."

"You're worried, aren't you?" Maddie asked, her blue eyes wide.

"I'm ... confused," Nick clarified. "Why isn't she down here with the rest of us?"

"Let's go look at her room," Aaron said. "Now you've got me wondering."

"Let's all go," Max said. "It will be like an adventure."

"I can't go on an adventure with my head pounding like this," Lauren said.

"Then stay here," Nick said. "I'm sure this is nothing. I just ... I want to make sure."

Maddie read the look on his face. Normally something like this wouldn't bother Nick, but he was still edgy after her misfortune in the mausoleum. He hadn't seen a thing but he'd believed Maddie when she said she had. If Cassidy was legitimately missing, there was a chance something horrible happened to her.

"I'll come with you," Maddie said, standing up. "I want to make sure Cassidy is okay, too."

"Come on, love," Nick said. "I promise we'll still have our afternoon together once we find her."

"I DON'T LIKE THIS," Aaron said, his gaze bouncing from one side of Cassidy's room to the other. "All her stuff is still here and yet she's nowhere to be found."

"Are we sure she's not out on the grounds somewhere?" Brian asked. "This is a big parcel. She could be taking a walk for exercise or something. She's an adult. It probably didn't occur to her to tell someone where she was going."

"I sent Miranda out to double check with the lawn crew," Aaron said. "I haven't heard anything back and I told them to alert me if anyone saw her this morning. There are too many of them to miss her."

Nick rubbed the back of his neck. "Marla, have you tried calling her?"

Marla shook her head and immediately started digging into her pocket. "That's a good idea." She punched Cassidy's number into the phone and held it to her ear. After a few seconds, she shook her head. "It's going straight to voicemail."

"Leave a message," Nick instructed. "Tell her to call you right away."

Marla nodded and when she was done leaving the message she turned to the rest of the group. "I'm usually the last one to overreact, especially when I'm not the one in trouble, but I'm kind of worried."

"How was she last night?" Nick asked.

"What do you mean?"

"We told them about the conversation we had on the patio yesterday," Aaron said. "They know that we gave Cassidy a hard dose of reality."

"*Your* reality," Marla countered. "I ... she was fine. We had a few drinks at the fair, but neither one of us was drunk. She was fine when I left her in the hallway last night. I swear."

"Are you sure she didn't decide to go home?" Max asked. "She is the outsider here ... even more than Marla. Maybe she had enough and left."

"Without her stuff?" Nick asked, gesturing around the room. "I'm no expert, but those look like expensive shoes."

"Cassidy wouldn't leave without telling anyone," Marla said. "This weekend wasn't exactly a dream come true for her, but it's not as if she was depressed."

"She seemed a little depressed to me," Brian said.

"You don't even know her," Marla said.

"I don't think you know her either," Brian said.

Nick raised his hand to cut off their argument before it got a chance to build too much steam. "We don't have time for this," he said. "I think we should split up and search the house."

"I think that's a good idea," Aaron said. "I'll take Brian with me.

Max, you know the house as well as I do. Why don't you take Marla with you?"

"I don't want to go with her," Max said. "I'll take Maddie."

"Maddie is staying with me," Nick said.

"Of course she is," Max said, sighing. "Fine. Marla, if you make my hangover worse by ... being you ... I'm going to gag you. I'm just giving you fair warning."

"I hate you," Marla said, flouncing out of the room.

"This really is turning into a crappy day," Max said.

"**THIS** HOUSE IS HUGE," Maddie said, running her hand over the wall as she trailed Nick down the hallway. "Where should we start looking?"

"I don't know," Nick said, his face serious. "I don't suppose ... ."

"What?"

"Is there any way to call your ghost here and ask her to help us?" Nick felt like an idiot for asking the question. He had no idea what was allowed on the ghostly plane, or how things worked in Maddie's world, but a bad feeling had been building in the pit of his stomach since the maid interrupted breakfast with news of Cassidy's disappearance.

"I don't think she has a cell phone," Maddie said. "I ... I'm sorry. It doesn't work that way."

"It's okay, Mad," Nick said, reaching over and giving her hand a reassuring squeeze. "It was a shot in the dark. I don't even know where to start looking here. She could be anywhere. I mean, for all we know, she could've fallen and hit her head."

"You don't believe that," Maddie said. "You're worried whatever was in the mausoleum with me yesterday attacked her."

"I'm not sure if that's what I'm worried about or not," Nick said. "I just ... this doesn't feel right to me. I don't know Cassidy as well as I should given the fact that I dated her for six months, but this doesn't seem like something she would do."

"I'm not saying this because I'm jealous you're worried about her, but ... um ... do you think she would hide to cause a panic? I mean, she seemed upset about the attention you were doling out to me yesterday."

Nick frowned. "You don't have anything to be jealous about."

"I know," Maddie said. "I ... that was the wrong word to use."

"If you had asked me three months ago if she was capable of something like that I would've told you no without even thinking twice about it," Nick said. "After the way she reacted when she found out I was going to break up with her, though, I'm just not sure."

"Well, we have to look for her either way," Maddie said pragmatically. "Neither one of us is going to be able to live with ourselves if we let it go and then something happens to her."

"Where do you suggest we start looking?" Nick asked.

"Why are you asking me? You're the police officer."

"And you're the one who is magic," Nick said.

"I ... magic?"

"I meant that in more ways than one, Mad," Nick said. "Is there some way you can, I don't know, find a mystical trail?"

"I've never tried before," Maddie admitted.

"Now seems like a great time to start."

Maddie nodded, turning back to the wall and screwing her eyes shut. She touched the wall, inhaling heavily as she tried to center herself. She internally said Cassidy's name over and over again, and then before she realized what was happening, she started walking.

Nick had no idea what was going on, but he knew enough not to speak in case he shattered the spell. He kept his eyes on Maddie as she navigated down the hallway. When she got to a spot where two hallways met, she tilted her head to the side before drifting down the corridor that led to the right.

Nick followed her, impressed with how intent she seemed. When she stopped in the middle of the hallway, though, he started to doubt what she was doing.

"There's something here," Maddie said finally.

As far as Nick could tell, the only thing there was a linen closet. "I don't think so, Mad."

Maddie ignored him and reached for the closet door. She expected it to be locked, but when the handle turned easily, she pulled it open and peered inside. Instead of a closet, though, she found herself staring down another hallway. This one was dark, though.

"What is that?" Nick asked, moving up behind her.

"I think we just found a whole other part of the house."

They exchanged a look and then Nick grabbed her hand. "You stay close to me, love."

"I'll be fine."

"I didn't say you wouldn't. Stay close to me. I don't want to be separated from you – and that doesn't just go for today."

"I'll be right beside you."

"For the rest of your life," Nick said, stepping into the bowels of the house.

16. SIXTEEN

"Do you think Aaron knows this is here?" Maddie asked, studying the walls as they shuffled through the dim space. "It doesn't look like anyone has been in here for years."

"I don't know," Nick said, keeping his eyes trained on the area in front of them while he pulled Maddie along behind. "I think it would be hard for him not to know about it."

"Why don't you think he mentioned it when we found out Cassidy was missing?"

"Maybe it never occurred to him that she could find the passage-way. The only reason we did is because you're ... you."

"Maybe," Maddie said. "I ... what's that up there?"

"I don't know," Nick said, increasing his pace when he caught sight of the lights Maddie was gesturing toward. When he got to the end of the hallway his eyes flew open as he realized what they were looking at. "That's our bedroom."

"I don't understand what this is," Maddie said, biting her lip. "I ... is this the other side of that big mirror?"

"I think so," Nick said, letting go of her hand so he could feel around the window. "I think it's one of those double-sided mirrors. You can see what's going on in the room from this side, but the people on the other side would be none the wiser."

"We're the people on the other side," Maddie reminded him. "We're the people who have been dressing and undressing in that room. We're the people who ... made love ... in that room last night."

"I know. If it's any consolation, I don't think anyone has been hanging around in here and watching us."

Maddie wanted to believe him, but she wasn't so sure. "Nicky, look at the floor."

Nick did as instructed, frowning when he realized what Maddie was directing his attention toward. "Someone has been in here," he said. "Those are fresh footprints, and they're not ours."

"You don't think ... ."

"Stay calm, love," Nick said. "We don't know anything yet. I ... ." He broke off when a glint of gold caught his attention out of the corner of his eye. "What is this?" He reached down and snagged the item off the ground, holding it up so he could study it in better light.

Maddie's heart lodged in her throat when she recognized it. "That's Cassidy's necklace."

"Are you sure?" Nick asked.

Maddie nodded. "She's worn it every day since I met her."

Nick turned, scanning the small alcove for another clue. After a few minutes, he gave up. "I think we should call Dale," he said, referring to his partner on the Blackstone Bay Police Department.

"Why?"

Nick showed the necklace to Maddie. "Because this chain is broken," he said. "It looks like someone ripped it off of her."

The seriousness of his words caused Maddie's stomach to flip. "Do you think ... ?"

"I don't know," Nick said, running his hand down the back of her hair. "I just know the longer we don't report Cassidy's disappearance the worse position it puts us in. We have to take this one step at a time, Mad. This is only the first step."

DALE KRESKIN LOOKED dubious as his gaze bounced from face to face in the library an hour later. "Are you sure she's really missing?

No offense, but from the look of most of you, you had a pretty late night."

"We're pretty sure," Nick said, holding his hand out to Kreskin.

"What is this?" Kreskin took the necklace and studied it. "Is this hers?"

Nick nodded.

"Is that her necklace?" Marla asked, moving up next to Kreskin. "Where did you find that?"

Nick exchanged a quick look with Maddie. "We found it in the hidden passageways upstairs."

"What passageways?" Brian asked.

"The ones that lead through the walls of the house and allow people to see right into our bedroom," Nick said, grimacing.

"Holy crap," Aaron said, leaning forward. "I ... dude, I haven't been in those passageways in years. I forgot all about them."

"Me, too," Max said, his face unreadable. "We used to play hide and seek in them all the time when we were kids. I haven't even thought about them in a really long time, though."

Marla made a face. "No, that's not true," she said. "I saw you go into one the other night. That's how I knew where to find the doorway."

A pall settled over the room.

"You were in there with Cassidy last night?" Nick asked, opting to take on Marla first. "Didn't you tell us that you guys came in from the fair, said goodnight to each other in the hallway, and then went straight to bed?"

"I ... um ... oh, fine," Marla said, making a face. "I knew the passageways were there and I wanted to see where they led. We weren't in there very long. We wandered around a little bit until we saw you guys in your bedroom and then we left."

Maddie's hand flew up to her mouth as her eyes widened. "You saw us?"

"Oh, don't get all high and mighty," Marla said. "You didn't even know we were there. It's not like we saw the actual event. We just saw the foreplay."

"Oh ... ." Maddie's cheeks burned as she fought off tears.

"You're a disgusting pig," Nick snapped, wrapping his arm around Maddie's shoulders. "Love, it's okay. Don't freak out."

"I can't believe you watched us," Maddie said. "That's such an invasion of privacy."

"We didn't go in there looking to spy on you," Marla said. "I was just exploring ... kind of like Nick was when he stripped you out of that dress." Marla's glare was malicious.

Maddie turned her head into Nick's chest, afraid to meet anyone's gaze in case she burst into tears. She felt violated.

"That is just unbelievable," Christy said, jumping to her feet. "How could you do that?"

"Oh, get over yourself," Marla said. "It's not our fault. It was an accident. Cassidy made me leave before we saw anything good. Personally, I wanted to see what Nick looked like without his pants on, but she was all shaken and ashamed."

"Well, I guess that makes one of you," Aaron said. "Seriously, Marla, what is wrong with you?"

"Hey, I am not the bad guy in this," Marla snapped. "We stumbled upon that little room accidentally. We left before we saw them actually do anything. I refuse to be ashamed."

"And that's why everyone hates you," Lauren said.

Kreskin held his hand up to still the argument. "Listen, this is all ... fascinating."

Nick shot him a look as he rubbed comforting circles on Maddie's back.

"It's actually deplorable," Kreskin said. "As horrible as it is, though, that's not our main concern right now. What happened after Cassidy made you leave?"

"Nothing," Marla replied, nonplussed. "We went back to the hallway where our rooms are located and said our goodnights."

"How was Cassidy when you left her?"

"She was ... sad," Marla said. "If you want to know the truth, I think seeing Maddie and Nick in a private moment made her realize that it really was over between her and Nick."

"I think the breakup should've been proof of that," Nick said, shifting so he could pull Maddie flush against his chest and soothe her. "You're the one who kept telling her she still had a shot. This is on you, Marla."

"I didn't do anything to her," Marla shot back. "Don't you even think about blaming me for this. If you hadn't broken her heart in the first place, none of this would've ever happened."

"Shut up, Marla," Christy said.

Kreskin pinched the bridge of his nose, frustrated. "Marla, was Cassidy wearing her necklace when you left the passageway together?"

Marla racked her brain. "I think so. I can't be a hundred percent sure, though. It's not like I was looking for it."

"If she didn't drop the necklace when she was in there with you, that means she went back on her own," Kreskin said, casting a sympathetic look in Maddie and Nick's direction.

"That means she could've been spying on us for hours," Nick finished, kissing Maddie's cheek. "Good grief."

"I'm sorry," Kreskin said. "There are no words for how sorry I am, in fact."

"I'm sorry, too," Aaron said. "I should've warned you guys about those passageways. I honestly forgot."

"Speaking of forgetting, how come you said you forgot about the passageways, but Marla claims she saw you going into them?" Kreskin asked, turning to Max.

Max looked caught. He glanced at Aaron for a moment and then sheepishly lowered his gaze. "I might have gone in to spy, too."

Nick growled, causing Max to take a step back. "I was not spying on you. I was actually going farther down the hallway because I wanted to spy on Aaron."

"Holy crap, dude," Aaron said, flabbergasted. "You were spying on me?"

"Is there something you want to tell us?" Lauren asked.

"Oh, gross," Marla said, wrinkling her nose. "I slept with you."

"I wasn't spying on Aaron for *that*," Max said, rolling his eyes. "I hid a fake snake in his bed earlier in the day yesterday. I wanted to watch him freak out."

"That was you?" Aaron asked. "I should've known. You used to do that to me when I was a kid all the time. I was scared to climb into my bed for a month straight."

"That's why I did it," Max said. "I thought it was a fun callback to when we were kids. I went into the passageway to see if I remembered how to get to your room. It had been a long time since I was in there and I didn't want to get lost.

"Anyway, after two tries I found your room, and I was going to go back and watch you freak out about the snake last night but ... well ... we got hammered instead and I forgot because I was so drunk," Max said.

"Dude, you're such an idiot," Aaron said. "I'm far too manly to be scared by a fake snake. I didn't even blink twice when I saw it."

"Is that because you were drunk?"

"No, it's because I was two seconds from passing out," Aaron countered, smiling. When the gravity of the situation washed back over him, though, he had the grace to look abashed. "I'm sorry. Now is not the time for this conversation."

"What do we do now?" Christy asked.

"There's not much we can do," Kreskin said. "Cassidy hasn't been missing for twenty-four hours yet and there's no law against a grown woman voluntarily going missing."

"What about the necklace?" Nick asked. "It looks like someone ripped it from around her neck."

"Does it?" Kreskin asked, arching an eyebrow. "How do you know it didn't just get tangled in her hair and break on its own?"

"I ... ." Nick broke off, unsure. Now that Kreskin voiced the question, he wasn't sure how to answer. "It still doesn't seem like her to just disappear."

"Maybe she didn't," Kreskin said. "We all know she's been having problems with your relationship with Maddie. Heck, everyone in town saw her hiding from you at the fair a couple weeks ago. People were talking about it for days.

"I know you don't want this brought up again, but maybe she snuck back into the passageway and spied on you and Maddie long enough to get really upset," he continued. "What she saw might have depressed her, or made her angry."

"I know it depressed me," Marla grumbled.

"Shut up, Marla," Nick seethed.

"There are a lot of options we need to consider," Kreskin said. "Cassidy could've been so upset by what she saw that she left and went home. I'm going to stop there when I'm done here and make sure that's not the case. She also could've just gone for a walk to clear her head."

"What if something happened to her?" Nick asked.

"What?" Kreskin asked. "My understanding of the situation is that everyone's time from last night is accounted for. You and Maddie were ... together ... and everyone else was down here drinking."

"What about Marla?" Lauren asked.

"I didn't do anything!"

"Until Cassidy has been gone for twenty-four hours, my hands are tied," Kreskin said. "There are no signs of foul play. There's nothing to indicate that something bad happened to her."

"But ... ."

"Nick, you're a police officer," Kreskin said. "You know the rules. All you have is a broken necklace and Marla's story that Cassidy was watching you and Maddie last night. That's nothing."

Nick knew he was right. Still, the unsettled feeling in the pit of his stomach was growing – and not just because Maddie was a mess. "So, we just wait?"

"That's all we can do," Kreskin said. "I'm sorry."

17. SEVENTEEN

"We're leaving this place right now," Nick said, storming into their bedroom and immediately heading toward the closet. "We're not spending another night in this house."

Maddie, her stomach weak, sank down on one of the armchairs on the far side of the room and watched him angrily start rummaging through the closet.

"Where is that garment bag you brought?"

When Maddie didn't immediately answer, Nick turned in her direction.

"What are you doing, Mad? Get packed. We'll be home in an hour. I'd rather deal with whatever that thing is in your house than deal with this ... crap."

"Our house," Maddie said, automatically correcting him.

"Our house," Nick said, his face softening. "I promise to start calling it 'our house' once I move in."

"Nicky, we can't leave," Maddie said, her voice low and plaintive. "You know it as well as I do."

"I know nothing of the sort."

"We can't leave until we find Cassidy," Maddie said. "She's still here somewhere. I can feel it. We can't just walk away. You'll hate yourself if you do."

"I don't owe that woman any loyalty," Nick said. "After what she did ... ."

"She did it to me, too," Maddie said.

Nick sighed, running his hand through his hair as he shook his head. "Love, I don't even know what to say about what Cassidy and Marla did. I am so sorry."

"Why? It's not your fault."

"Isn't it? You didn't even want to come here this weekend," Nick said. "I was the one who pressured you into this. You would've been perfectly happy staying home and just seeing these guys at the fair. I should've listened to you."

Maddie licked her lips, considering her words carefully. "You didn't ask me to do anything unreasonable," she said. "I think you've been going out of your way to do everything for me since we got together. I don't blame you. I've been ... scared ... and unsure of myself.

"The thing is, Nicky, you can't protect me from the world," she continued. "You made the right choice when you asked me to come here. I need to put myself out there more. You're my world, but you can't be everything to me at every moment of every day. It's not possible."

"Maddie, I love you," Nick said. "The fact remains that I pressured you to come here. You have every right to blame me for all of this."

"That seems like a waste of time," Maddie said. "You didn't do this to us, Nicky. Marla and Cassidy did."

Nick pressed his lips together as he watched her. She was paler than he liked, and her face was drawn. There was no hint of playfulness on her features, and that realization made him inexplicably sad. He moved over to her and knelt in front of her, placing a hand on her knee to offer her comfort. "What are you feeling about what Cassidy did?"

Maddie shrugged noncommittally.

"Don't do that, Mad," Nick said. "We promised we were going to be truthful with each other from here on out. No more secrets. I know what Marla told us had to shake you."

"I honestly don't know what to think," Maddie said, reaching over so she could brush her fingers against the side of his face. He turned his mouth so he could kiss her palm, but otherwise remained still. "I know I shouldn't be embarrassed. I'm not embarrassed about what we were doing. That's not it. It still feels like someone … took something from us."

"What?"

"I don't know," Maddie said. "It was just a … violation."

"It was definitely a violation," Nick said. "They didn't take anything from us, though. They can't. You can't give Marla the power to upset you, Mad. That's what she wants. Marla has nothing to do with our relationship. You and I are … forever. Marla isn't even a consideration for the next five minutes."

"Can I ask you something?"

"Always."

"How do you feel about what they saw?"

"I don't know," Nick said. "I don't think I'm as upset as you are. Personally, I think I was on top of my game last night."

Maddie barked out a hoarse laugh. "That's an interesting way of looking at it."

"You were on top of your game last night, too."

"That doesn't make me feel any better," Maddie said.

"I know," Nick said, sighing. "I guess that I feel … unsettled. It's not what they saw us doing, though, that's bothering me. I'm more upset that someone was watching us and I didn't know. I'm supposed to protect you."

"You can't protect me from something when you don't know it's happening," Maddie said. "Don't be ridiculous."

"I know that in my head," Nick said. "My heart is a different story. My heart belongs to you, and when you hurt, I hurt. I saw what Marla's admission did to you. It … scared me."

"Because I fell apart?"

"You didn't fall apart," Nick said. "You were just ... thrown."

"No, Nicky, I fell apart there for a few minutes," Maddie said. "Don't make excuses for me. I was mortified that everyone knew what we were doing."

"I hate to break it to you, love, but they knew what we were doing before Marla told them what she saw," Nick said. "They've been trying to get me to tell them what you look like naked for two days."

"That's just guy stuff. That's not the same thing."

"I don't want you to ever feel ... unsafe ... when we're together," Nick said. "I can't help but feel my armor has a big chink in it now because I failed to protect you from Marla."

"You can't protect me from Marla," Maddie said. "It's time I started protecting myself from Marla. You're right on that front. The good news is that you're right on just about every front this morning. We were both on our games last night."

Nick smiled, lifting his hand and pushing Maddie's hair away from her face. "There's my girl."

"We still can't leave," Maddie said. "No matter how angry you are with Cassidy, you're not going to be able to let this go. Our best shot of finding Cassidy is to stay here, so that's what we're going to do."

"Okay," Nick said, giving in. "We're hanging a blanket over that mirror, though."

"Oh, absolutely," Maddie said. "We also need to go back to the cemetery."

"What? Why?"

"I need to talk to Rose," Maddie said. "If anyone can help us find Cassidy, it's her."

"Do you think whatever that thing was in the mausoleum is what took Cassidy?"

"I don't know," Maddie said. "Even though I heard noises in there, I can't say with any amount of certainty that the entity had corporeal form."

"You need to dumb that down for the jock," Nick said.

"I heard noises, but I can always hear noises when it comes to ghosts," Maddie said. "In my head, I thought there was something physical in that room. That doesn't mean there was. I was terrified. My mind was a blank."

"So ... I don't know what that means."

"Most ghosts aren't capable of affecting physical surroundings," Maddie said. "Take my mother, for example. She can pop into my room – and we've had a talk about that, by the way. She's decided she's not going to do that once we're officially living together. She doesn't want to risk seeing something that would kill her a second time."

Nick chuckled softly. "That's good to know. Thank you."

"Anyway, Mom can watch things, and she can talk to me, and she can understand what's happening around us, but that doesn't mean she can open a door, or touch me in a way that I can feel."

"That would be nice, wouldn't it?"

"For my mother, yes," Maddie said. "The idea of other ghosts being able to touch me freaks me out a little bit."

"Wait a second," Nick said, his expression thoughtful. "If ghosts can't affect physical beings, what went after you and Maude in the house?"

"That was something else," Maddie said. "I've been giving it some thought, and I think it was a poltergeist."

"How is that different from a ghost?"

"A poltergeist is kind of like an angry spirit," she said. "They're all rage and no soul. They don't know anything but anger. They can funnel that anger into physical manifestations."

"How many poltergeists have you encountered?"

"Only two," Maddie said. "I'm also starting to think that's what was in the mausoleum."

"You're not sure, though, are you?"

Maddie shook her head. "I'm not sure of anything right now. I need more time to investigate."

Nick rubbed his chin thoughtfully. "What are the odds that a poltergeist would show up at your house and then follow you here?"

"I don't think that's what happened," Maddie said. "I think the poltergeist lives here and somehow was drawn to me at home. I don't know why yet, but I do think it's the same poltergeist. Sometimes they can just feel when someone is psychic."

"Is there any way to communicate with a poltergeist?"

"No," Maddie said. "Most of them exist until the object of their rage disappears."

"Do you mean until the object of their rage dies?"

"Sometimes."

"Okay," Nick said, rubbing his hands against Maddie's thighs. "Here's what's going to happen: We're going to snuggle here for five minutes because I have an overwhelming urge to hold you. Then we're going to hang a blanket over the mirror before we head down to the cemetery."

"Nicky, can you put the blanket up first?"

"You've got it, love."

"ARE you sure this is a good idea?" Christy asked, keeping her voice low as she grouped in a corner downstairs with Maddie and Nick. "What am I supposed to tell people when they ask where you are?"

"Tell them we went for a walk," Nick said. "Do not mention the cemetery. I don't want anyone going down there looking for us."

"Just tell them we're looking for Cassidy," Maddie suggested. "They're not going to find that suspicious."

"I guess not," Christy said. "Are you sure you don't want me to go with you?"

"I'm sure I want you to stay up here and keep an eye on Marla," Nick said. "I don't trust her and you're the only other person here who I know hates her as much as I do."

"Everyone here hates her," Christy said. "Don't kid yourself."

"Fine," Nick said. "Everyone hates Marla."

"That would be a great sitcom," Maddie mused.

Nick grinned. "It would be the top-rated show in Blackstone Bay, that's for sure."

"I'm glad you're feeling better," Christy said, patting Maddie's arm. "I'm really sorry about what happened."

"I am, too," Maddie said. "It happened, though, and dwelling on it isn't going to do me any good. I have to put it behind me."

"That's a healthy attitude, in theory," Christy said. "I'm not sure how practical it is in reality, though."

"I can't think about that right now."

"We hung a blanket over the mirror," Nick said.

"I don't blame you," Christy said. "I would ask to switch rooms."

"This is our last night here regardless," Nick said. "I'm not moving all of our stuff. Once sunrise hits, we're out of here."

"We're staying until we find Cassidy," Maddie corrected.

"Mad, I don't want to burst your bubble, but there's an off chance we might never find Cassidy," Nick said.

His words were sobering. "What?"

"We don't know where she's at," Nick said. "We don't know that seeing us together didn't ... cause her to snap."

"What are you suggesting?"

"Oh," Christy said, realization dawning. "You think she might have killed herself, don't you?"

"I think that's a possibility," Nick said. "That doesn't explain the broken necklace, though. I know Kreskin said that it could've accidentally fallen off, but I don't believe that. I think someone ... or something ... took her from that room."

"Something?" Christy asked, arching an eyebrow. "Like the something that went after Maddie in the mausoleum?"

"Exactly," Nick said. "That's why we're going down to the cemetery. We need you to hold things together up here while we're gone."

Christy clicked her heels together and mock saluted. "You can trust me, sir."

"You're cute," Nick said. "I'm serious, though. Don't tell anyone where we're going and keep your eyes and ears open. We need you with all of your faculties intact ... so no drinking."

"Honey, if I never drink again it will be too soon," Christy said. "Trust me on that front."

"Just be careful," Nick said. "Maddie is my priority, but I'm partial to you, too."

"Right back at you, handsome."

18. EIGHTEEN

"Absolutely not." Nick crossed his arms over his chest and fixed Maddie with a firm look. "You are not going into that mausoleum alone."

"I'm not asking to go in alone," Maddie said. "In fact, I'm terrified to go in there alone. I'm asking you to go in there with me and let me look around to make sure there's nothing ... freaky ... in there. Then I want you to leave me alone so I can talk to Rose."

"Why can't I be in there when you're talking to her?"

"I don't think she likes you."

Nick stilled. "Why not? I'm a charming man. Just because I can't see her, that doesn't mean I can't schmooze her."

"You're the most charming man in the world," Maddie said, poking his ribs playfully. "I don't think she dislikes you because you're not charming. I think it's because you're a man."

"Oh," Nick said, straightening. "I guess I can live with that."

"Awesome," Maddie said.

Nick linked his fingers with hers and walked into the mausoleum first. He made sure the door was wide open so there wouldn't be any mistakes, and then he proceeded to search the small room. "Cassidy isn't in here," he said.

"Did you expect her to be?"

"No. It would've made things easier."

"It would have," Maddie agreed. "Since when do we do things the easy way, though?"

Nick shrugged. She had a point. "Do you see anything else in here?"

Maddie glanced around, leading Nick completely around the room for another turn before she was satisfied she was alone. "It's not here."

"I'm still not keen on leaving you alone in here, Maddie."

"You're going to be right outside the door," Maddie pointed out. "You'll hear if I need you."

"I ... promise me you'll be careful."

"I promise."

Nick pulled her close and gave her a warm hug. "I love you."

"I love you more," Maddie whispered, giving him a soft kiss.

"That's not possible, love."

ONCE MADDIE WAS ALONE she found she wasn't sure how to proceed. She'd never tried to summon a ghost before. Rose was different than the other spirits she'd encountered. Instead of trying to cling to the mortal plane – or being anxious to cross over to the other side – she was stuck in limbo. It made her ... unpredictable.

"Rose?"

Maddie waited to see if the woman would appear. For some reason she had the distinct feeling that she was being watched – and not in a creepy way. It felt as if Rose was present, but apparently she wasn't thrilled with the idea of showing herself.

"I know you're here, Rose," Maddie said, hoping her voice didn't betray the edginess clouding her heart. "I really need to talk to you. If you could just spare a few minutes, I promise I'll be quick."

Maddie heard Rose before she saw her. "I thought you were dead."

Maddie swiveled, following the sound of the voice until her eyes landed on the filmy woman in the corner. "Hi."

"Seriously, I thought you were dead," Rose said. "What are you doing back here?"

"I need to talk to you," Maddie said. "Something bad has happened."

"Yeah, you almost died."

"Worse than that," Maddie said.

"What's worse than that?"

"Have you seen anything ... weird ... around here this morning?"

"Well, I did see a blonde woman hanging around a mausoleum so she could talk to a ghost."

Maddie made a face. "You have an interesting personality."

"Right back at you."

"One of the women staying up at the house with us has disappeared," Maddie said. "You haven't seen her, have you?"

"I haven't seen anyone but you," Rose said. "My social life isn't exactly buzzing these days."

"What about the ... thing ... that was in here with me yesterday?" Maddie asked, changing tactics. "Have you seen that again?"

"No."

"Do you know what it is?"

"Evil."

Maddie sighed, frustration bubbling up. Getting Rose to open up was like pulling teeth. Since she was dealing with a ghost who didn't have any teeth, it was starting to feel as if she was climbing a mountain. "Rose, I'm really tired," Maddie said. "I've spent the past three days sharing a roof with the woman my boyfriend used to sleep with and the pain in the ass who has gone out of her way to make my life hell for as long as I can remember. I need your help."

"Maybe I need your help," Rose countered.

Maddie was surprised. "How can I help you?"

"I've been thinking about what you said. I want you to help me pass over to the other side. I don't know what will be waiting for me there, but it has to be better than here."

"If I help you, will you help me?"

Rose nodded

"Okay," Maddie said. "I need some information first, though. How did you die?"

NICK WAS restless as he paced outside of the mausoleum. The walls of the small building were thick, and even with the door open he couldn't hear Maddie. He'd stuck his head in briefly, relieved to find her holding a one-sided conversation, and then stepped back out. He'd promised to give her space to work, and he had every intention of keeping that promise.

"What are you doing out here?"

Nick jumped when he heard Max's voice, swiveling quickly. "I'm ... um ... what are you doing out here?"

"I'm looking for Cassidy," Max said, his face unreadable. "You didn't answer my question."

"That's what I'm doing, too," Nick said.

"Alone?"

"Maddie is in the mausoleum," Nick said, opting not to lie.

"Why would she possibly go back in there?" Max asked. "After yesterday, I would think she'd be terrified of that place."

"That's not how Maddie rolls," Nick said. "When she's scared of something she likes to meet it head on. She's hanging out in there until she isn't frightened." As far as lies go, it was a lame one. Nick couldn't think of a better story on the spot, though.

"I guess that makes sense."

Thankfully for Nick, Max was dealing with a hangover so he wasn't exactly quick on the uptake. "Did you find anything while you were searching?"

Max shook his head. "The truth is, I was looking and yet I wasn't just looking. Does that make sense?"

"Not without the proper context," Nick admitted.

"I didn't realize that it would be so hard to come back here," Max said. "It's been almost six years since I've seen this place, and for a long time I considered it my home even though it never really was."

"What do you mean?"

"I'm not sure you'll understand this ... heck, I'm not sure I even understand it," Max said. "The thing is, I've always been jealous of Aaron. I was worried I would still feel that way when I came back."

Nick furrowed his brow, confused. "You guys have been best friends for twenty years. If you're jealous of him, you've done a good job of hiding it."

"I'm not saying I sit in a little room and hate on him," Max said. "It's just ... my mother was a servant in that house. Aaron always treated me as an equal, and his father didn't treat me like I was anything other than an equal, but his mother always looked down her nose at me.

"Even though I lived under the same roof for years, I always knew that living below the main floor wasn't the same as living above the main floor," he continued. "I was a kid, and I shouldn't have grasped that people have certain stations in life, but I always did."

"I don't know what to say, Max. I never thought about you having to deal with stuff like that. I guess I was never a very good friend to you."

"Don't beat yourself up," Max said. "I like you, but it's not like we were close. Your life was all about Maddie even back then. She was your best friend."

"Does Aaron know you feel this way?"

"We've never talked about it," Max said. "It makes me feel ungrateful to complain about stuff like this when he's been such a good friend to me. He never once talked down to me, even though he would've been allowed to because that was his house and I was just a temporary guest."

"Aaron isn't the type of guy to look down on someone," Nick said. "He's a good guy."

"He is," Max said. "I've never understood why he moved away, though. I've always loved that house. I thought he did, too. It's almost as if he hates being here, though. I think that's why he invited everyone to stay here this weekend. He didn't want to be alone."

Nick stilled, an idea niggling the back of his brain. "When you were living here as a kid, did you ever see anything ... abnormal?"

"I once saw Aaron's mother throw a thousand-dollar tea set away because one cup had a tiny chip," Max said.

"That's not what I'm talking about."

"What are you talking about?"

"There's a cemetery on the property," Nick said. "It would make sense that maybe there were other things – ghosts even – hanging around. Did you ever see anything like that?"

"Are you asking me if I ever saw a ghost?"

"I ... yes."

"No," Max said. "No offense, man, but I don't really believe in that stuff. Do you believe in ghosts?"

"I believe in a lot of different things," Nick said. "I don't think it's outside the realm of possibility that the human soul exists beyond this world."

"I guess," Max said, shrugging. "I can honestly say that I've never seen a ghost, though. Sorry."

"Don't worry about it."

The two men lapsed into silence for a little bit. Finally, Max broke it. "I'm going to head back up to the house. Do you want me to wait for you?"

"I'm just waiting for Maddie," Nick said. "We won't be long."

"Okay. I'll see you up there."

"MY LIFE WASN'T happy even when I still had it to live," Rose said, her face taking on a far off quality. "My husband wasn't interested in being married to me, and the only reason he did it is because he was expected to deliver a male heir.

"The times were different then," she continued. "Women were expected to work in the house, never outside of it, especially when they were well off like we were. I didn't want to marry anyone when I was younger. I wanted to be a nurse. That's all I ever wanted. Still, I was raised to listen to my father, and when he told me I was expected to marry Jim, I did what I was told.

"I wouldn't say that our life together was happy, but it wasn't terrible either," Rose said. "Once I gave birth to a son, Jim pretty much left me alone. I wasn't a priority to him and he wasn't a priority to me. We even had separate bedrooms."

"That sounds awful," Maddie said.

"When you have responsibilities, awful is a state of mind," Rose said. "I did the best I could, and when I announced to my husband that I wanted to be a nurse, he didn't put up a fight. I expected him to, but he seemed just as excited to get me out of the house as I was to leave.

"The last few months of my life were the best months I ever had," she said. "I was working sixty hours a week, and yet I was never tired. I found a purpose for myself that didn't revolve around running the staff or mothering an entitled child.

"Oh, don't look at me that way," Rose said. "I loved my son, but he was a brat. His father gave him everything he wanted, and that kid learned at a young age that all he had to do to get some attention was to pitch a fit."

"I wasn't judging you," Maddie said hurriedly.

"It doesn't matter," Rose said. "I'm getting off track anyway. You want to know how I died. This is just a long way of telling a short story. One night a few weeks before Christmas I came home from a particularly late shift at the hospital. I was the only one up in the house. Everything else was dark.

"I took a shower. I had a late snack. Then I went to bed," she said. "I was sound asleep when it happened. Something woke me up. I wasn't sure what it was right away. I was groggy and confused when I opened my eyes.

"Everything was still dark around me, and when I lifted my hands I found that a pillow was pressed against my face," Rose said. "I have no idea who was in the room with me. I never saw a face, and I never heard a voice. I struggled to fight whoever it was off, but it was too late.

"After about a minute and a half, I just ... drifted away," she said. "It was almost peaceful."

"That's horrible," Maddie said.

"In the grand scheme of things, there are worse ways to go," Rose said. "I know you're going to try to help me pass over, but that's all I have for you to go on. I don't know who killed me."

"Do you think it was your husband?"

"That would be my best guess, but there really is no way for me to know," Rose said. "I'm not sure he had the courage to kill anyone. Can you help me without knowing who killed me?"

"I hope so," Maddie said. "I need to give it some thought, though. While I'm doing that, I need you to do something for me."

"You want me to look for the missing girl, don't you?"

"That's exactly what I want you to do."

"What do I do if I find her?"

"Come find me," Maddie said. "Come find me right away. I don't care if I'm around a bunch of people. Find me and I'll find a way to get away from everyone. I can't explain what's going on, but I feel like I'm running out of time. If we don't find Cassidy in the next few hours, I'm really afraid that we never will."

"We're working together on this now," Rose said. "If the last months of my life taught me anything it's that I can do whatever I put my mind to. I'm putting my mind to this."

"Good luck."

"To you, too."

"I think we're both going to need it," Maddie said.

19. NINETEEN

"Do you think Rose is going to be able to find Cassidy?" Nick asked, his fingers linked with Maddie's as they walked back toward the main house.

"I think she's got a better shot at it than we do."

"Why aren't you more excited then?"

"Because I need to find a way to put Rose to rest," Maddie replied. "She's so sad."

"It sounds like she's more disengaged than sad," Nick said. "If I had to guess, her life was just as depressing as her after-life. Wow, there's a sentence I never thought I'd say."

"Look at all the conversational topics I've brought into your life with my return," Maddie teased.

"You've brought a lot more to my life than that, Mad," Nick said. "You brought sunshine and light back into my life, too."

"Oh, so schmaltzy." Maddie pinched his cheek and shook it.

"So pretty," Nick said, dipping his mouth to hers.

"Well, I'm glad to see that your ex-girlfriend's disappearance and probable death hasn't gotten in the way of your romantic weekend," Marla said, appearing on the back patio as the couple approached.

"I'm glad to see you've taken the time to fix yourself a drink instead of looking for your friend," Maddie shot back.

Nick's eyebrows flew up his forehead, surprise washing over him. Maddie was rarely catty, but she was in fighting form right now.

"Hey, I'm trying to make myself feel better," Marla said. "My best friend is probably dead in a ditch somewhere."

"How did she get in a ditch?" Nick asked.

"I ... you know what I mean."

"Yeah, have another drink," Nick said, rolling his eyes.

"Why don't you go on another romantic walk?" Marla shot back.

"We weren't on a romantic walk," Nick said. "We walked down to the cemetery to look around in case Cassidy was down there. We wanted to check the mausoleum. The door sticks, in case you've forgotten. We just wanted to make sure she didn't accidentally get shut in there."

"Oh," Marla said, her face softening. "I'm guessing you didn't find her."

"It doesn't look like she's been down there," Nick said.

"What are we supposed to do?" Marla asked.

"Keep looking."

"SO, tell me what you found down at the cemetery," Christy said, settling next to Maddie on the library couch.

In an effort to give Maddie and Christy some privacy, Nick left them in the library to talk while he corralled everyone else on the back patio. He was hoping they could brainstorm and think of another lead, or that's what he said. Maddie thought he was really trying to give her time to decompress after her conversation with Rose, and she loved him for it.

"Not much," Maddie said. "Cassidy definitely wasn't down there."

"What about the ghost?"

"Her name is Rose."

"Was Rose down there?"

"She was," Maddie said. "We had a long talk."

"About?"

"She's agreed to help us," Maddie said. "She's going to search the grounds and house for Cassidy, and if she finds her, she's going to come and tell me right away. So, if you see me kind of staring off into space, that's probably what I'm doing. You might need to supply me with a distraction."

"Don't worry about it," Christy said. "I haven't flashed anyone in years. I figure I'm about due."

Maddie faltered. "I ... you're joking, right?"

"No, I often go around showing random people my boobs," Christy deadpanned. "Of course I'm joking."

Maddie exhaled slowly. "That's good to know. I was worried you were trying to pick up a date in the worst way possible."

"Oh, see, you're getting to be funny and snarky these days," Christy teased. After a few moments, her face shifted from amused to serious. "Does Rose want you to help her pass over once she finds Cassidy?"

"She does," Maddie said. "That's a problem all on its own, though."

"Why?"

"She doesn't know who killed her," Maddie explained. "All she knows is that she woke up to a pillow pressed over her face and she died about a minute later."

"She was smothered?"

Maddie nodded.

"Shouldn't her husband have noticed that happening? He was in the same bed with her, after all. Shouldn't we assume he's the culprit?"

"We are assuming he's the culprit, even though Nick says it's never smart to lock in on a suspect without absolute proof," Maddie said. "The problem is, Rose says she and her husband had separate bedrooms."

"Well, that's a little depressing," Christy said. "Who wants to get married so they can sleep alone?"

"It sounds to me like she didn't want to get married in the first place," Maddie said. "I had to read between the lines, but I think it was a business deal more than anything else. She said her father just told her she was marrying Jim Denton one day and that was it.

"It also doesn't sound like their marriage was a happy one," she continued. "Once she gave birth to a male heir, though, I think he pretty much left her alone."

Christy snorted. "Of course he did. He was too busy fornicating with the staff to pay attention to his wife."

Maddie was confused. "What do you mean?"

"Oh, come on," Christy said. "You've never heard the stories about Jim Denton?"

"He was a little bit before my time," Maddie said. "How do you know about him?"

"I've already told you, I love to gossip," Christy said. "It's a family thing. My mom loves to gossip and my grandmother does, too. My grandmother knew Big Jim pretty well, in fact."

"Big Jim?"

"I think he nicknamed himself," Christy said. "With all the sex he was having, I'm guessing he was trying to prove something to everyone who would give him the chance."

"Tell me about him," Maddie said.

"Why?"

"It might help me help Rose."

Christy shrugged. "Keep in mind that this is all coming secondhand from my grandmother, so take it with a grain of salt."

"I'm used to grandmother gossip," Maddie said. "Did you forget who I live with?"

"Your grandmother is fat with the gossip," Christy said, chuckling. "I'll bet she has some good stories about Big Jim. From the sounds of it, he tried to tap anything with a pulse and he didn't care who knew about it."

"That must have been rough on Rose," Maddie mused.

"The thing is, Big Jim liked to put in public appearances in town," Christy said. "He was the one who always lit the Christmas tree every year. He was the one who lit the bonfire at the Fourth of July party ...

and Memorial Day party ... and Halloween party ... and the Easter party."

"I get it. He liked to be the center of attention."

"That's just it," Christy said. "He liked to be the center of attention, but he never did any of those things with his wife on his arm. I guess it was a running joke that someone was going to end up with a pinched rear end whenever he was in the general vicinity."

"That must have been a sign of the times," Maddie said. "He wouldn't be able to get away with that these days."

"I think Big Jim got away with just about whatever he wanted to get away with," Christy said. "In addition to romancing some of the women around town – whether they were married or not – the rumor is that he was also a frequent guest in the servants' quarters."

Maddie frowned. "Seriously?"

"My grandmother says he had heavy turnover with the maid staff because they either had to put out or get out."

"That is despicable," Maddie said.

"That was a sign of the times, too," Christy said. "He fired women because they wouldn't sleep with him, and even the ones who did sleep with him weren't known to hang around long because he only liked to dip his wick for so long before he got bored. I think he had a six-month cycle, too."

Maddie made a face. "That isn't funny."

"It was a joke," Christy said, poking her in the side. "Don't worry. Nick is infatuated with you. There's no way he'll ever get bored."

"Of course he won't," Maddie sniffed.

"Your self-esteem is getting better," Christy said. "That's a good thing. Anyway, where was I?"

"The maid staff."

"Oh, right," Christy said, rubbing her hands together as she gleefully got to the meat of the story. "Big Jim essentially hired a new maid every six months until one woman – and I wish I could remember her name, but I can't – changed all of that. Apparently she was some dark-haired beauty. She supposedly looked like a model."

"Did he fall in love with her?"

"That's the rumor," Christy said. "For once in his life Big Jim wasn't the one in control of a relationship. This maid stole his heart and his ... you know."

"I'm pretty sure I do know," Maddie said, her tone dry.

"The affair went on for years," Christy said. "The maid wanted to move upstairs with Big Jim and claim her rightful place in the house – or at least what she thought was her rightful place – but Big Jim refused because he knew that would be the talk of the town."

"I thought he didn't care what the town thought."

"He didn't. People thinking he's having sex with the maid is different than the maid moving into his bedroom, though. That would've been pretty hard to explain in the big money circles he was running in."

"I guess that makes sense," Maddie said, rubbing her neck thoughtfully. "What happened?"

"Things remained as they were for another couple of months," Christy said. "I think there were rumors that the maid was pregnant, but I'm going to have to check with my grandmother to see if that's true. I could just be making that up in my own head because I watch so many soap operas."

Either scenario wouldn't surprise Maddie, but she forced her face to remain neutral while Christy finished her story.

"When Rose Denton died it was a shock to the whole town," Christy said. "The woman wasn't well known by the residents, but she was well liked. Most people thought she got the short end of the stick – maybe in more ways than one – when she married Big Jim. When she started working at the hospital, most people thought she was gearing up to leave him."

"I don't think that's true," Maddie said. "She made it sound like she was perfectly fine to let him do his thing as long as he left her alone to do her thing."

"That's probably true," Christy said. "If the maid showed up pregnant, though, I don't think Rose could've pretended she didn't know what was going on. That might have been too much for her to deal with."

"I'll ask Rose if the pregnancy rumors were true next time I see her," Maddie said. "Tell me about the maid. Whatever happened to her?"

"Rose's death was never ruled a murder," Christy said. "That's important to note because if she was murdered, Big Jim obviously would've been a suspect."

"Obviously."

"The death was ruled natural. I think it was deemed a heart attack. Rose was put to rest in the family mausoleum, and Grandma said that everyone expected Big Jim to put in the proper mourning time and then officially move the maid into his bedroom."

"That didn't happen?"

"No," Christy said. "Instead, the maid disappeared about five months after Rose died. Some people thought she moved away because she gave Big Jim an ultimatum to marry her and he said no. Other people think he killed her because she was putting too much pressure on him. I'm not sure anyone knows the truth about what really happened to her."

"You know, if this maid was as adamant as you say she was about marrying Big Jim and claiming what she thought she deserved, she might have been the one to kill Rose," Maddie mused. "Big Jim was probably scared to divorce Rose because he didn't want his reputation to take a hit. In his mind, having sex with the maid and letting his wife ignore him was probably the best of both worlds."

"That's an interesting thought," Christy said. "Smothering someone does sound like the way a woman would commit a murder instead of a man."

"I need to find out this maid's name," Maddie said. "Do you think you can call your grandmother and find out who she was?"

"Sure," Christy said. "Keep in mind, though, this was forty years ago. I love my grandmother, but sometimes I think she can't remember my name."

"It's the only option we have right now," Maddie said. "I'll give Granny a call, too. Even if she doesn't know the name of the maid, she's been hanging out with the Pink Ladies all weekend. I'll bet one of them knows."

"That's a good idea," Christy said. "If you do find the maid, what are you going to do?"

"I have no idea right now," Maddie said. "I'm just playing this by ear and taking it one step at a time."

"And you're feeling better about the whole Marla-and-Cassidy-spying-on-you-and-Nick-while-having-sex thing, right?"

"I wouldn't say I'm feeling better, but crying about it isn't going to do me any good," Maddie said. "It is what it is, and Nick brought up a good point."

"What's that?"

"We were both on top of our games last night," Maddie said, winking.

"Maddie Graves, I swear," Christy said. "Every time I think I have you figured out, you turn around and surprise me."

"And don't you forget it."

20. TWENTY

Maude wasn't thrilled to see Maddie's name pop up on her cell phone when it began to ring. "Good grief."

She was gathered around Beverly's kitchen table with a handful of friends, and they were halfway through a euchre tournament and barely into a fresh fifth of bourbon. She considered ignoring the call, but she figured Maddie was the type to worry enough to stop whatever she was doing and drive into town to check on her. No one wanted that.

"I'm fine and I'm still alive," Maude said, rolling her eyes for her friends' benefit as she answered the phone.

"Good," Maddie said, and for a moment Maude could practically picture her annoyed face from ten miles away. "I thought you were going to ignore my call there for a second."

Maude scowled. She loved Maddie more than life itself, but that psychic streak she boasted was downright annoying sometimes. "Would I do that?"

"Yes." There was no hesitation on Maddie's part.

"Well, as you can hear with your own ears, I'm fine," Maude said. "There's no reason to worry about me."

"As much as I love you, I'm actually not calling to check up on you," Maddie said. "I need some help."

Maude made a face. "Help? From me? I'm actually really busy right now."

"Doing what?"

"Um ... we're planning a charity drive," Maude said.

"With bourbon and cards?"

"Stop doing that," Maude hissed. "You know I don't like it."

"Granny, I'm not asking you to go anywhere or stop what you're doing," Maddie said. "I need some information from you on Rose and Big Jim Denton."

Maude stilled, surprised. "Why are you asking questions about them?"

"Well, for starters, I ran into Rose while I was here."

"But she's ... oh," Maude said, getting up from the table. "I'll be right back, ladies. Take a break. No one touch that glass of bourbon. I'm not done with it."

Maude secluded herself in Beverly's den, closing the door to cut off errant eavesdroppers, and then sat down. "Okay. I'm alone now. Has she been up there this whole time?"

"Yes," Maddie said. "Did you know her very well?"

"I knew her, but I wouldn't say I knew her well," Maude said. "She was a good woman. She definitely deserved better than the likes of Jim Denton. I don't understand why she's still hanging around. She died in her sleep."

"She was smothered in her sleep," Maddie corrected.

"She was? Who did it?"

"She doesn't know," Maddie said. "Christy and I were talking, and she told me about Big Jim's history."

"You mean the fact that he humped anything that moved?"

"Yes ... and don't say 'humped.' It grosses me out."

"Do you think Big Jim killed Rose?" Maude asked, ignoring Maddie's prudish comment. "I wouldn't put it past him."

"He's on the top of my suspect list, but Christy mentioned something about one particular maid who spent years with Big Jim," Maddie said. "She said that this maid wanted to marry Big Jim, but Rose was standing in her way."

"Oh, you're talking about Rosario," Maude said. "Yeah, I remember her."

"Rosario what?"

Maude racked her brain. "I think her last name was Torres. She turned up out of nowhere one day. No one could figure out why a woman like her would end up in a place like Blackstone Bay."

"Because she was Hispanic?"

"Don't get all high and mighty," Maude chided. "It was a different time. Blackstone Bay was all white. Heck, it's still mostly all white. It wasn't a racist thing. It was a culture thing."

"No one knows where Rosario came from?"

"No," Maude said. "There were rumors about her departure, though. Apparently she just took off in the middle of the night. Some people thought Big Jim killed her because she was pregnant and he didn't want her to ruin his reputation."

"What do you believe?"

"Big Jim was an ass," Maude said. "I don't know that he had the stones to kill someone, though. He thought he was enough of a big muckity-muck to get away with anything. If Rosario really was pregnant, I think Jim would've found a way to take care of the kid and her."

"What about Rose? Do you think he would've killed her? Rose said they had separate bedrooms and they pretty much did whatever they wanted and led separate lives."

"I think Jim had the best of both worlds," Maude said. "Rose not only looked the other way where his infidelities were concerned, but she encouraged him to get his rocks off with other women just so she wouldn't have to touch him."

"Did you ever meet Rosario?"

"A couple of times," Maude said. "She was a real ball buster. You would think I would like that in a person, but she had a sneaky quality about her that I just couldn't stomach."

"Meaning?"

"She was just full of herself."

"Do you think she could've killed Rose?"

"I wouldn't put it past her," Maude said. "What are you going to do to help Rose?"

"Whatever I can," Maddie said. "Listen, something else is going on up here." She told Maude about the past few days at the Denton mansion. When she was done, Maude was flabbergasted.

"Holy wiggle worms," Maude said. "Do you think Cassidy is dead?"

"I don't know," Maddie said. "I ... that's not the feeling I'm getting. Rose is going to see if she can find her. For now, though, we're waiting."

"You be careful, Maddie girl," Maude said. "It sounds like things could go from bad to worse up there before you even realize what's going on."

"I'm being careful. We're coming home tomorrow regardless."

"What about the ... thing ... in the house?"

"I think the thing is up here," Maddie said. "I think it's a poltergeist. I don't know why it found me at home, but I'm pretty sure this is where it lives."

"What does Nick think about all of this?"

"Nick is struggling with it the same way I am," Maddie said. "It's a lot to grapple with."

"It's definitely a lot to grapple with," Maude said. "Keep me in the loop if something happens. And, Maddie girl, I love you."

"I love you, too, Granny."

"I'm going to stop loving you if you don't stop calling me that," Maude grumbled, although she didn't mean it.

"WELL, if what Maude says is right, that changes things, doesn't it?" Christy said, pouring herself a drink and offering one to Maddie.

"I thought you were done drinking for the rest of your life?"

"We both knew that wasn't going to stick," Christy said, unruffled. "I need something to soothe my nerves. Do you think Rosario killed Rose and then someone turned around and killed Rosario?"

"I think that someone killed Rose, and Rosario is looking like a better suspect than Big Jim right now," Maddie said. "We don't have any proof that Rosario is dead."

"We don't have any proof that she's alive either."

That was a good point. "I just don't know," Maddie said. "I'm hoping to get a chance to talk to Rose again tonight. If we're lucky, she'll find Cassidy and then find me."

"Are you feeling lucky?"

"I've been feeling lucky ever since I got back to town," Maddie said. "Let's hope it holds."

"What are you two gossiping about in here?" Marla asked, poking her head into the library and glancing around disdainfully.

"We're just talking about where Cassidy might be," Maddie said. That wasn't a total lie. It wasn't the complete truth either, though.

"Oh, don't pretend you care," Marla said, sauntering the rest of the way into the room and striking a pose next to the couch. "If Cassidy is dead, that makes your life a heck of a lot easier, doesn't it?"

Anger boiled in the pit of Maddie's stomach. "How can you even say something like that?"

"Because it's the truth," Marla said.

"What's going on in here?" Nick asked, appearing in the doorway. His gaze bounced between Maddie and Marla nervously. "Marla, why don't you go and spread your light and joy to everyone else out on the patio?"

"Why don't you butt out," Marla suggested, wrinkling her nose. "Maddie and I were just having a little discussion about how her life is going to be so much better now that Cassidy is probably dead."

"Shut your mouth," Nick snapped.

Christy reached over and grabbed his arm, shaking her head as she watched Maddie. Maddie didn't miss the gesture, but she couldn't spare time to think about it because she was about to explode.

"You're just so ... awful," Maddie said, glaring at Marla. "You're not happy unless you're making everyone else miserable. Why is that?"

"I'm not the one throwing a party because my rival is dead," Marla shot back.

"Cassidy isn't my rival," Maddie said. "Cassidy is a sad woman who had her heart broken. If you think I'm happy about that, you're wrong. I feel for her. I really do. I never wanted her to get hurt in all of this."

"That didn't stop you from stealing her boyfriend, did it?"

"I didn't steal Nick," Maddie said, her blue eyes flashing. "I came back to town to build a life for myself. Did I think Nick was going to be part of it? I didn't know. I would be lying if I said I wasn't hoping for it, though.

"The thing you don't seem to understand is that I've always loved Nick," she continued. "He's always been my whole heart. Before you even start in on your crap about me leaving town, you're right. I shouldn't have left. I was dealing with some stuff then and I handled it terribly. I'm not proud of it. If I had it to do all over again, I would do it differently.

"I still didn't steal Nick from Cassidy," Maddie said. "If I'd never returned to town, Nick was still going to break up with her. It probably would've happened sooner than it did, in fact."

"You don't know that," Marla said. "Nick could've fallen in love with Cassidy."

"No, he couldn't have," Maddie said, her face plaintive. "He was never going to love her. It's taken me a long time to come to grips with certain things, but I know that Nick loves me. I also know that I love him. We're meant to be together.

"That doesn't mean I want Cassidy hurt, and I especially don't want her dead," Maddie said. "I'm sick of it, though. I'm sick of all of it. I'm sick of your glares and Cassidy's pouting. I'm sick of you whispering about me behind my back. I'm especially sick of you keeping Cassidy's hopes up through lies. Even if Nick and I break up tomorrow, he's not going back to her.

"Enough is enough, Marla," Maddie said. "I'm starting to think everyone else is right. This isn't about Cassidy at all. This is about your crush on Nick. You've always wanted him. You convinced yourself I was the reason you couldn't have him. The truth is, you can't have him because you're mean and awful and he would never love someone like that."

"You're just so full of yourself," Marla spat.

"I'm also done playing this game," Maddie said. "I'm not scared of you. I'm done trying to hide my happiness because it might upset others. I have everything in my life that I've ever wanted. I'm going to enjoy it. You might want to try and find some happiness for yourself because I'm not going to let you tear me down ever again. I'm done."

Marla opened her mouth to speak, but no sound came out. Maddie's diatribe had clearly taken the wind out of her sails. Instead of saying something hateful, Marla surprised everyone by turning on her heel and flouncing out of the room without a backward glance.

Once it was just the three of them, Christy broke into applause. "That was awesome. Good job, Maddie."

Maddie glanced up at Nick, worried he was going to be disappointed with her minor fit. The broad grin on his face told her he was feeling something entirely different. "What?" Maddie asked, suddenly feeling self-conscious.

"You're my hero, Maddie Graves," Nick said, swooping closer and pulling her in for a hug. "I love you more than anything in this world."

"I love you," Maddie said, burying her face in his neck.

"I'm going to leave you two to your mutual love association," Christy said, heading for the door. "You have twenty minutes until dinner. You'd probably better make it count."

"We have our whole lives," Nick said, rubbing the back of Maddie's head as he kissed her neck. "We have forever."

21. TWENTY-ONE

"So, does anyone want to tell us what happened in that library?" Aaron asked, his gaze bouncing between Maddie and a murderous-looking Marla as they settled around the dinner table.

"Nothing," Marla said, crossing her arms over her chest.

"Oh, please," Christy said. "Maddie laid down the law and finally put Marla in her place. It was glorious."

"It was nothing of the sort," Marla said.

"Oh, it was," Christy countered.

"I'm sorry I missed it," Lauren said. "What did Maddie say to her?"

"She just told her she'd had it with Marla building herself up by tearing others down and that she was going to ignore her from now on and focus on being happy," Christy said. "She also told her that she didn't have a shot with Nick and she could suck it."

"I didn't say that," Maddie said.

"You did say it, just not in that way," Christy said. "I embellished a little. I was putting my spin on it."

Nick grinned as he slung an arm around the back of Maddie's chair. "My girl was pretty hot in there ... in more ways than one."

"And just when I thought I'd beaten my hangover you made me sick to my stomach again," Brian teased. "Nice job."

Nick shot him a thumbs-up. "I aim to please."

Over a dinner of red wine-infused steaks, baby red potatoes, and Caesar salad, everyone did their best to relax and enjoy the night. It was hard with the pall of Cassidy's disappearance hanging over them.

Max and Aaron started regaling everyone with stories about their childhood, and when one particular story touched on Big Jim Denton, Maddie saw her opening.

"I've heard a lot about your grandfather," she said. "What was it like to grow up with him in the same house?"

"He died when I was fifteen," Aaron said. "There are a lot of tall tales about Gramps, but I'm not sure how many of them are really true. If you believe my mother, none of them are true. I think she just didn't want me to act like him, though. If you ask my father, they're all true. He thinks Gramps was a larger-than-life character straight out of a movie."

"What do you think?" Christy asked.

"I think that my grandfather was very nice to me," Aaron said. "I also think he was a terror when it came to the staff and, from what I can tell, he was a righteous dirtbag when it came to women."

Well, this was almost too easy. "I ... um ... heard about your grandfather's reputation when it came to women," Maddie said. "Do you think that was all true?"

"Oh, it was true," Aaron said. "Even when he was older he was still handsy. Finally, my father had to tell him to stop groping the maids. Dad was terrified we were going to be sued. The way Gramps did things in the seventies and eighties was not the way my dad wanted to do things."

"What did your mother think?" Lauren asked, helping Maddie without even realizing it.

"Mom wasn't Gramps' biggest fan," Aaron said, smirking. "She had to be nice to him, though. She didn't have a choice. The big house was his, and if she wanted to live in it, she had to put up with his ... proclivities. It killed her, though.

"Mom loves this house," he continued. "It's a status symbol to her. While Gramps was in the big room, though, she had to either put up or shut up. When Gramps died, I think she was secretly happy."

"That's horrible," Lauren said.

"Like I said, I loved Gramps," Aaron replied, nonplussed. "I can see why he pissed people off, though. As a teenager, all the life advice he gave to me seemed like a great idea in theory. You can imagine my surprise when it didn't pan out in real life."

Max snorted. "I particularly liked it when you walked up to that woman at the mall and told her that you were rich so she should strip," he said. "What were you, fourteen?"

Aaron blushed. "Right around there. The woman was thirty. He told me that's how you get women," he said. "I took it literally when I probably shouldn't have."

Everyone chuckled, the idea of a fourteen-year-old boy hitting on a grown woman entertaining everyone. As amused as she was, Maddie wanted to get more dirt on Big Jim.

"What about your grandmother?" Maddie asked. "How did she put up with your grandfather?"

"I don't know," Aaron said. "The truth is, no one ever really talked about her much while I was growing up."

"That's sad," Christy said. "You don't know anything about her?"

"I know that she didn't like Gramps very much and she was considered a bad reflection on the family when she decided to get a job as a nurse," Aaron said. "The interesting thing is, she sounds like one of the only members of my family who was truly a good person."

"Did your dad ever talk about her?" Nick asked.

"Not a lot," Aaron said. "I think he respected her, though. He never talked about her in front of Gramps. I got the feeling it was a sore subject. He did mention her a couple of times, and it always felt like he had a lot of regrets where she was concerned."

"Meaning?"

"Dad admits he was a bratty kid," Aaron said. "Despite how entitled my mom felt – and that's exactly the way she wanted to raise me – Dad put his foot down with a lot of her weird ideas.

"She wanted me to go to private school, but Dad said there was nothing wrong with public school, and she wanted to force me to date in ... higher class ... circles," he continued. "Dad said the only thing I was going to find there was misery. That really set her off because that's how they met.

"Anyway, Dad always said that Grandma was right about the way we lived our lives," Aaron said. "He thought the Denton name was all flash and no substance. He said if Grandma survived longer she might've been able to turn our family into something truly great."

Rose was growing in Maddie's estimation by the moment. "She sounds like an interesting lady."

"She does," Aaron agreed. "I never got to meet her, and I think I probably lost out on that front."

"Did your mother like her?" Lauren asked.

"My mother never met her," Aaron said. "I doubt they would've liked each other, though. Heck, if Grandma survived longer, Dad probably wouldn't have married Mom and I wouldn't even be here."

"What do you mean by that?" Nick asked, genuinely curious.

"If you believe family gossip, which I take with a grain of salt given my family, Grandma was making noises about taking Dad and moving out of the house when she died," Aaron said.

"Why?"

"Apparently Gramps was fornicating with one of the downstairs maids."

Max perked up. "I've never heard this story."

"It was quite the scandal at the time," Aaron said. "The maid wanted to move into the big bedroom with him and everything."

"What about your grandmother?" Lauren asked.

"They had separate rooms," Aaron said. "I believe, once my father was born, they never touched each other again."

"That must have been hard on your grandfather," Marla said. "No wonder he went looking for love in other places."

"I think it was a mutual decision," Aaron said. "I'm pretty sure my grandmother didn't even want to marry Gramps. It was one of those business mergers. Her father was rich and my great-grandfather was rich. They put their heads together and married their kids off as a way to get even richer."

"That's a little depressing," Brian said. "If you're going to get married, I think love should be a necessary prerequisite."

"Love is overrated," Marla said. "Most marriages were arranged by parents for centuries. You didn't hear about those people getting divorced. Marrying for status and money is the only way to go."

"Oh, with a romantic streak like that I can't believe you're not married," Max deadpanned.

"Go back to the maid," Christy said. "You dropped that story. How come she didn't marry your grandfather after your grandmother's death? If my grandmother is to be believed, she was pregnant."

"Oh, wow, is that true?" Lauren asked.

"That's another one of those family rumors that's survived over the years," Aaron said. "I never got up the guts to ask my father if it was true but once, when my mother had a few too many gimlets, I asked her.

"She said that the woman purposely got pregnant to trap my grandfather and when he refused to acknowledge the baby and marry her she cut her losses and left," he said.

"That's quite the story," Nick said. "Do you think it's true?"

Aaron shrugged. "There's a lot of stuff in my family that's shrouded in secrecy," he said. "I do think it's funny that my mother fought so hard to get into the big room, and then six months after getting it she decided to split her time between here and Florida."

"Why is that such a big deal?" Maddie asked.

"Because of the ghost," Aaron said, chuckling harshly.

Maddie stilled, her heart flopping as she risked a glance at Nick. He looked interested, too.

"What ghost?"

"My mother is convinced that this place is haunted," Aaron said. "She swears up and down that she's seen plates hit walls without anyone being there to throw them, and she says she's heard people screaming in the night even though no one is there."

"Have you ever seen a ghost?" Maddie asked.

"Nope. There have been times when I could swear I was being watched, though," Aaron said. "Don't laugh, Max. I told you this when I was a kid."

"And I laughed back then, too," Max said. "I lived here for several years and I never saw – or heard – anything like that."

"I didn't say my mother wasn't crocked," Aaron said. "I just think she likes attention. She's kind of like Marla that way."

Marla scowled. "You suck."

Nick rubbed the back of Maddie's neck thoughtfully. "Aaron, are there any other passageways in the house beside the ones we found on the second floor?"

"Not that I know of," Aaron said. "To be fair, though, I wasn't supposed to know that one existed. My mother was convinced I'd get into trouble if I could hide in there on a regular basis."

"Why do they exist at all?"

"I have no idea," Aaron said. "My guess is that my grandfather wanted a way to come and go from various beds and he wanted to be able to do it without anyone knowing what he was up to."

"The passageway we found doesn't go to the basement, though," Nick pointed out.

"Huh," Aaron mused, rubbing his chin. "I never really thought about that. You know, the room you and Maddie are staying in was my grandmother's room. Maybe, before she moved out of his room, Gramps had someone else in that room. I really have no idea."

"We're staying in your grandmother's room?" Maddie asked, surprised.

"Yeah. Why? Is that a problem?"

"No," Maddie said, shaking her head. "I was just curious." Out of the corner of her eye, she saw a hint of movement at the far end of the room. At first, she thought it was a member of the kitchen staff, but when she focused her full attention on the area next to the drink cart, she saw Rose floating there. The woman's face was hard to read, but Maddie couldn't help but wonder if she'd garnered a modicum of respect for the grandson she'd never met thanks to the turn in the conversation.

"I'm going to get a drink," Maddie said. "Do you want something, Nicky?"

"I can get it," Nick said. "I ... ."

"I've got it," Maddie said forcefully, clasping his hand for emphasis.

Nick scanned her face for a hint. "Okay."

Maddie started moving toward the cart, and in an effort to distract everyone else from what she was doing, Nick opted to keep the conversation going. "Do you think your grandmother knew your grandfather was cheating on her?"

"Gramps never went out of his way to hide it," Aaron said.

Maddie tuned the rest of the conversation out as she closed in on Rose. She was careful to keep her back to prying ears and her voice low. "Did you find Cassidy?"

"He grew into a better man than he probably should have," Rose said, ignoring Maddie's question and focusing on Aaron. "His father sounds like he grew to be a better man than I expected, too."

Maddie didn't reply.

"For some reason, knowing that makes me feel better," Rose said. "I don't know why."

"Because it means your legacy lived on in this house long after you died," Maddie whispered. "Did you find Cassidy?"

"Who is that other boy?" Rose asked. "The one sitting next to Aaron. Why do I feel like I should know him?"

"He lived here when he was a child. His mother was a maid."

Rose studied Max for a few moments, her face conflicted. "I ... oh, no."

"What?" Maddie asked, alarmed.

"I'd recognize those eyes anywhere."

Maddie didn't get a chance to ask the next question on her lips because at that exact moment the power blinked out and plunged the house into darkness.

22. TWENTY-TWO

"What's going on?" Christy asked, her shaky voice belying her nerves.

"The power went out," Marla replied, nonplussed.

"Oh, really, I thought your mouth sucked up all the energy in the world and plunged us into a black hole," Christy shot back.

"Marla is the black hole," Lauren said.

"You're both ... dumb," Marla said.

"Nice one," Brian said. "You have a gift for comebacks."

"Why isn't the generator kicking on?" Max asked.

"That's a good question," Aaron said. "The better one is why did the power go out in the first place?"

No one got a chance to answer because the room lit up briefly, a terrific bolt of lightning cutting across the sky and illuminating the room through the glass patio doors. A loud rumble of thunder followed it.

"Well, I guess that answers that question," Aaron said.

"It still doesn't explain why the generator hasn't kicked on," Max said.

"Where is the generator?" Nick asked.

"It's on the east side of the house," Aaron said.

"Do you think you can find it?"

"Yeah. I'll go look, although I have no idea how to fix it when I get there," Aaron said.

"I'll go with you," Nick said. "I'm not a handyman, but I'm pretty handy."

"That's the word on the street," Christy quipped, her voice shrill. "Is anyone else worried that the power went out right after Aaron told us his mother thought the house was haunted?"

"Don't freak yourself out," Nick said, scraping his chair against the floor as he pushed it out so he could stand up. "Aaron, we should go out this door here and walk around the house. We'll probably be able to see better than we could inside."

"Okay," Aaron said.

"Maddie?"

"I'm here."

"I'll be right back," Nick said. "Stay here. Don't go wandering around. Promise me."

"I promise."

"What about the rest of us?" Marla asked. "Can we walk around?"

"I recommend you walk around outside and stand by a tree," Nick said.

"That would be stupid," Marla scoffed. "Trees are more likely to be hit by lightning."

"Exactly," Nick said.

"What do you want us to do?" Brian asked.

"Wait here," Nick said. "No one should go wandering around the house. It's too dark, and the house is too big. I don't want anyone else ... getting lost. Everyone needs to stick together."

"I agree," Christy said. "We should all stick together."

"Max, there are some candles in the buffet by that wall next to Gramps' portrait," Aaron said. "Just in case we can't get the generator up and running, it might be helpful to have candles so we can see ... something ... when we get back."

"I'm on it."

.   .   .

"I FOUND THE CANDLES," Max announced.

"Do you want an award?" Marla asked.

"Do you want to shut it?" Max shot back.

"Calm down," Lauren said. "There's no reason for everyone to get all worked up. It's just a storm."

"And a ghost," Christy said.

"We don't know it's a ghost," Lauren said. "That would be kind of cool, though."

"I always thought I wanted to meet a ghost," Christy lamented. "Apparently I was wrong."

Maddie couldn't hide her smile, even as she searched the darkness for a hint of Rose. Maddie had no idea if the skittish ghost hung around once the power vacated the premises, but she was dying to know what the woman was talking about when she commented on eyes she would never forget. Was she talking about Max? It was possible. She was talking about him moments before she made the ominous statement. There were several other options at the table, though, and she couldn't be sure it was Max who threw Rose.

"Does anyone have a lighter ... or matches?" Max asked.

"I do," Brian said. After bumping into no less than three chairs during his trek across the room, he finally joined Max by the buffet. Within seconds, the room was brighter – although only marginally – and the panic that had settled over the room lifted somewhat.

"Oh, well, now I feel better," Christy said.

Maddie scanned the room, hoping Rose was merely hiding in the shadows. She was disappointed when she didn't find her. Where could she have gone?

"Maddie, do you want to sit down and take a load off?" Max asked, smiling. "There's no sense of standing down there all night."

"Sure," Maddie said, shooting him a smile and heading in his direction. "I'm sure it won't take Aaron and Nick long to get the power back up."

"I'm sure, too," Max said.

. . .

"IT'S REALLY COMING DOWN," Nick said, pushing his hair back from his forehead so he could peer into the rain easier. "How far away are we?"

"We're close, but I can't remember exactly what window the generator is by," Aaron said. "I ... oh, here it is."

Nick and Aaron approached the boxy contraption so they could study it.

"I have no idea how this thing even works," Aaron admitted. "This is when having servants your entire life really comes back to haunt you."

"Maybe it's just out of gas," Nick suggested, kneeling next to the generator and unscrewing the tank lid. He slipped his finger inside and felt around. "It feels full to me, although I can't see to be sure."

"What else could it be?"

"Give me a second," Nick grumbled, feeling around the generator. "I don't suppose you have access to a flashlight out here, do you?"

"We probably should've thought about that inside," Aaron said.

"Thanks for the news tip."

"Sorry," Aaron said. "I ... oh, wait. My cell phone has one of those flashlight apps. Hold on." He rummaged in his pocket, and after fiddling with the phone for a moment, the screen flared to life. Aaron pointed it at the generator. "Where do you want me to point it?"

"Right here," Nick said. "Okay. Hold it steady. Let me look for a second."

"YOU PROBABLY DON'T REALIZE this, but I always had a crush on you in high school," Max admitted, reclining in the chair next to Maddie and sipping his beer.

"You're just saying that," Maddie said. "I'm pretty sure I would've noticed something like that."

"Really? I think the only thing you noticed in high school was Nick."

"That's not true."

Max arched a challenging eyebrow.

"Fine," Maddie said, blowing out a sigh. "It's probably true. Don't take it personally. I was really shy in high school. Nick was the only one I felt comfortable around."

"How come?"

Maddie shrugged. "I don't know," she said. "We just bonded at an early age. He always knew what I was thinking. He always knew how to make me laugh. We always fit together."

"It's such a waste, though," Max teased, the candle on the table flickering as he shot Maddie a roguish grin. "I'm much better looking than Nick."

"You're definitely handsome," Maddie conceded. "I don't think anyone is more handsome than Nick, though."

"Ugh, you two are just so ... gross," Max said, laughing. "Seriously, though, haven't you ever considered that you're just with Nick now because everyone always thought you belonged together?"

Maddie stilled. "No."

"Well, think about it, Maddie," Max said. "Life is often a self-fulfilling prophecy. Look at Aaron. He's successful because everyone in his family was successful. He's never actually done anything on his own. He's a Denton, though, so his life turned out like this because there was no other way it could turn out. He was born into absurd wealth and that led to success.

"With you and Nick, everyone kept telling you for years that you belonged with him," he continued. "People were beating you over the head with it. What's the first thing you did when you got home? You reunited with Nick. I don't think that means you belong together. I think it means you're scared to give anyone else a chance."

Maddie was starting to feel uncomfortable. "I ... um ... I love Nick."

"Of course you do," Max said. "You're best friends. I love Aaron, too. He's my best friend. That doesn't mean I'm in love with him. I'm not saying you and Nick aren't going to live happily ever after. I'm just questioning whether you're really in love with him."

"I am," Maddie snapped, her tone dark.

Max held his hands up in mock surrender. "I'm just kidding." He smirked. "You're so easy. You thought I was hitting on you, didn't you?"

"No," Maddie said hurriedly, although she wasn't sure that was the truth. "I knew you were screwing around."

"I just want to mess with Nick," Max said. "In case you haven't noticed, I have a particular knack for getting under people's skin."

"Maybe that's your self-fulfilling prophecy," Maddie suggested.

"Maybe," Max said. "I happen to think I'm destined for another form of greatness, though."

"I'M NO EXPERT, but it looks like someone cut a wire," Nick said, running his fingers over the ragged edges of the exposed copper wiring.

"Are you serious?"

"Yeah," Nick said. "I don't think this happened by accident."

"Can you fix it?"

"Not in the rain," Nick said. "I might be able to rig it if we had electrical tape, but it's too wet and I would be worried it would catch on fire."

"Yeah, let's not burn the house down," Aaron said. "What do you think we should do?"

"I think we should go back inside," Nick said. "We can build a fire in the library and everyone can hunker down there for the night."

"Sleep there?"

"I'm not going to lie, Aaron. This bugs me," Nick said. "Why would someone purposely sabotage the generator?"

"I don't know," Aaron said. "You seem to think something nefarious is going on, though. Why do you think someone would do that?"

"Maybe they knew the storm was coming," Nick suggested. "I haven't been paying attention to the news, but someone else could've been. Maybe they were hoping the power would go out and that would serve as a way for them to ... do something. We've all been distracted today because of Cassidy's disappearance."

"Did you hear back from Kreskin?"

"He checked her house. She hasn't been there."

"Do you think she's dead?" Aaron asked.

"I don't know," Nick answered. "I can't figure out what the motive would be."

"Maybe she killed herself."

Nick would be lying if he said the possibility hadn't occurred to him. "Maybe. If she did, though, where is her body?"

"Maybe she did it in the woods," Aaron suggested. "Heck, for all we know, she went for a walk in the woods and got lost."

"This is Michigan, not Alaska," Nick said. "Even if she got lost, if she walked in a straight line for three hours she would've come across something. A highway ... a gas station ... something. Cassidy would've called out here to let us know she was okay."

"You're starting to freak me out," Aaron said. "What do you think happened to her?"

"I think someone took her."

"Why?"

"If you can answer that question for me, we'll be able to solve the riddle," Nick said.

"What riddle?"

"Who has the most to gain from Cassidy's disappearance?"

"Well ... ." Aaron broke off, pondering the question. "The easy answer is you and Maddie."

Nick made a face. "Excuse me?"

"She was making things uncomfortable for you," Aaron said. "I'm not saying you did it. I don't believe that. In the grand scheme of things, though, you and Maddie had the most to gain."

"Cassidy wasn't a threat to Maddie and me," Nick said.

"I didn't say she was," Aaron said. "She was being pathetic and annoying, though."

Nick sighed, running his hand through his sopping hair. "I feel bad for how I treated her. I do. I'm sick of the looks, though. I didn't mean to hurt her emotionally and I certainly didn't physically hurt her."

"I know. I saw the look on your face when you found out Marla and Cassidy were watching you and Maddie. You were surprised. I never suspected you."

"I just can't figure out how taking Cassidy benefits anyone. She doesn't have money. She doesn't have power. She's just a normal woman."

"What about Marla?"

"You think Marla did something with her?" Nick asked.

"I think that Cassidy disappearing has given Marla a lot of attention," Aaron said. "Maybe Cassidy threatened to tell someone that Marla was spying on you guys and things got out of hand. It might've been an accident."

That was an interesting thought. "I guess," Nick said. "That doesn't feel right to me, though."

"What does feel right?"

"I don't know," Nick said, pushing himself to a standing position. "All I know is that we can't do anything out here right now. Let's go back inside. Maybe if we all put our heads together we can figure this out."

AFTER MAX'S WEIRD COMMENTS, Maddie decided to distance herself from the boisterous man. He was probably joking, Maddie told herself. She wasn't familiar with his sense of humor. Some people simply found odd things funny. Max was probably one of them.

After begging off on further conversation by saying she was going to get a drink, Maddie found herself wandering back in the direction of the drink cart. Her mind was busy with endless possibilities. The only thing she knew with any certainty was that she needed to talk to Rose.

Almost as if on cue, Rose appeared in the doorway that led from the dining room into the adjacent hallway. "Come with me," she said.

Maddie glanced toward the far end of the table where Brian and Max were regaling Christy, Lauren, and Marla with some long-forgotten football story. She wasn't sure leaving was a good idea, but she was sure Rose was her only chance of finding Cassidy.

Maddie knew she was running out of time. She had to trust the woman. There was no other way.

Maddie considered telling Christy she was leaving the room, but she knew that would draw unnecessary attention to herself. Instead, she wordlessly slipped away from her friends and followed Rose into the darkness.

23. TWENTY-THREE

"Did you find Cassidy?" Maddie asked, following Rose down the hallway while keeping her fingertips against the wall so she could maintain her bearings. It was hard to see her given the eerie darkness, but the frequent bursts of lightning gave Maddie enough glimpses to stay on track.

"I found a girl," Rose said. "She's been ... hurt."

Maddie swallowed hard, dread washing over her. "Where?"

"Close," Rose said. "Follow me."

"WE CAN'T GET the generator going," Aaron announced, walking into the dining room and shaking his head to dislodge the rainwater.

"Eww," Marla shrieked, jumping up from her chair. "You got me wet."

"You'll live," Aaron said.

"Where is Maddie?" Nick asked, immediately searching the room for her.

"She was just here," Christy said, scanning the dim dining area. "She was down there talking to Max for a little bit. Then Max came down here and told us a story. I don't know where Maddie is. Maybe she went to the bathroom."

Nick's heart rolled painfully. She'd promised to stay in the room. Why would she possibly leave? He knew the answer before he internally finished voicing the question. Rose.

"Where is Max?" Aaron asked.

"Maybe he went after Maddie," Lauren suggested. "He does know the house really well."

Something niggled the back of Nick's brain. "He does know the house," he said. "He knows it as well as you do, Aaron. Maybe even better."

"What are you getting at?" Aaron asked.

"He lied about being in the passageways," Nick said. "The only reason he owned up to it was because Marla saw him and she called him on it in front of everybody."

"So what?" Aaron asked, getting defensive. "He only went in there so he could play a prank on me."

"Do you believe that?"

"I found the rubber snake in my bed."

Nick tilted his head to the side, considering. "He lived in the servants quarters with his mother for years," he said. "You yourself said that you thought the passageways were originally put in so your grandfather could ... fornicate ... with the help. There has to be a way to move from floor to floor in the passageways."

"I also told you I wasn't even born when all of that was going on," Aaron said. "It was just a rumor that Gramps put in those passageways so he could slip downstairs without being noticed. I don't know it for a fact."

"It makes sense, though," Nick said. "What if Max discovered how to get into the passageways from downstairs?"

"So what if he did?" Aaron pressed. "That doesn't mean he did anything. What would be his motivation for hurting Cassidy? You said yourself that no one here has a motive ... except for you and Maddie."

"I'm glad to see someone has finally come to their senses and agrees with me," Marla said.

"Shut up, Marla," Nick and Aaron snapped in unison.

"Maddie and I went back down to the mausoleum this afternoon," Nick said. "We wanted to look around and be sure that Cassidy didn't accidentally find her way down there and lock herself in."

"Crap. I didn't even think of that," Aaron said. "You obviously didn't find her."

"We didn't," Nick agreed. "Max showed up down there, though."

"So?"

"We had a little talk," Nick said. "He said a few odd things."

"He always says odd things," Aaron said. "That's what he does."

"This was odder than usual," Nick said. "He talked about being jealous of you. He talked about loving the house and wanting to be part of the family when he was a kid. He talked about ... people having stations in life."

"That doesn't mean anything," Aaron said. "I ... he said he was jealous of me?"

Nick nodded. "Was Max with you the entire night when you got drunk?"

"Yes," Aaron said triumphantly. "We were all together the whole time."

"Well, not the whole time," Lauren said, casting an apologetic look in Aaron's direction. "He disappeared for about a half hour. I only remember because he'd been rubbing my shoulders and I was hoping he would come back and finish the job."

"I don't remember that," Aaron said, biting his lower lip. "That still doesn't mean anything. Why would he want to hurt Cassidy?"

"Maybe he didn't want to hurt her," Nick said. "Maybe she just got in his way."

"His way for what?"

"Where was Cassidy's necklace found?" Nick asked, forcing himself to remain calm.

"In front of the window that looks into the room you're sharing with Maddie," Aaron said.

"Maybe Max wanted to see what was going on in our room, too," Nick said. "Maybe finding Cassidy there was a surprise. Without a lot of time to think, maybe Max overreacted and ... did something to Cassidy because he needed her to be quiet."

"You're reaching," Aaron said. "Why would Max want to spy on you and Maddie? He'd just spent the previous two nights having sex with Marla. Sure, he said it was uninspired and she's a dead fish in bed, but they still had sex. He's not some sort of sick voyeur."

"I am not a dead fish!"

Everyone ignored Marla.

"He's always had a crush on Maddie, though," Christy said.

Nick stilled. "What?"

"He has," Christy said. "He's always thought she was pretty. He was going to ask her out until you and Brian came to blows. That didn't stop him from trying to spy on her in the woods, though. He even admitted it when we were drunk last night."

"Oh, yeah, he did," Lauren said. "I forgot about that."

Nick clenched his jaw, frustrated. "Why didn't you tell me this?"

"What does it matter now?" Lauren asked. "You and Maddie are obviously together. It's not like he thinks he can get between you."

"That's not what he was saying to Maddie," Marla said.

"What do you mean?" Nick asked, snapping his head in Marla's direction.

"I heard them talking while you guys were outside," Marla said. "Max was giving Maddie an earful about how she didn't really love you and she was only with you because everyone thought you should be together. He was yammering on about self-fulfilling prophecies and how Aaron was only successful because of his family's money and Maddie was only with you because everyone expected it of her."

"Why didn't you say something?" Nick asked.

"Because I was hoping he would convince her to dump you," Marla said. "Trust me. You could do much better."

Nick slammed his hand down on the table, furious. "Where is Maddie? Did she leave this room with Max?"

"I didn't see Maddie leave the room," Christy said. "I did see Max leave, though. He seemed distracted."

"Dammit," Nick said, grabbing a candle from the center of the table and stalking toward the hallway.

"Where are you going?" Aaron asked.

"To find them."

"WHERE ARE WE?" Maddie asked. She'd been following Rose for five minutes, and while the ghost wasn't exactly chatty, she hadn't been silent either.

"This is the heart of the house," Rose said.

"I don't know what that means," Maddie admitted.

"Here," Rose said, gesturing toward a blank wall.

"What am I looking at?"

"There's a door behind there," Rose said. "We're in the servants' quarters. No one lives down here now. All of the staff lives offsite. This part of the house is empty now, but it's where everything happened when I was living here."

Maddie's heart went out to the woman. "Is this where your husband came to ... ?"

"Have sex with the maid staff? Yes."

"How do you feel about that?" Maddie asked, using her fingertips to search the wall for a door. "How do I open this?"

"There's a button on the side of the framework just there," Rose said, pointing. "Push it up."

It took Maddie a moment to find the button, and when she did an audible click filled the air before the wall seemingly gave way and fell open. "What's in here?" Maddie asked.

"What you've been looking for."

Since it was dark beyond the wall, Maddie had no choice but to feel her way through. Surprisingly, when she moved a few feet inside, she realized that emergency lights lit the way down a narrow hallway. It wasn't bright, by any means, but it wasn't dark either. The lights looked to be running off of batteries.

"Do these passageways go throughout the entire house?" Maddie asked.

"Jim had them installed because he thought they would hide his actions," Rose said, leading Maddie down the hallway. "That was before he stopped caring about hiding his actions."

"Were you ... jealous?"

"No. I was relieved. The man was insatiable. He only cared about his needs, though. Mine were never a consideration."

"Did you ever love him?"

"I never did anything but loathe him," Rose said. "I know people in town gossiped about us. I know they thought I was jealous and sad. That wasn't the case, though."

"Were you really thinking of packing up your son and leaving?"

"No," Rose said. "As much as I hated Jim, he was a relatively decent father. He loved our son. We came to an agreement. I ignored what he was doing and he let me do what I wanted to do. It wasn't a happy marriage, but it was a comfortable compromise."

"Tell me about Rosario."

"She was ... bigger than life," Rose said. "I knew she was trouble the second we hired her, but I figured she was Jim's problem. She came to this house with plans to seduce him. It wasn't a hard task. All she had to do was smile at him, spread her legs, and he was hers.

"She played things differently than the other women, though," she continued. "She teased him ... and she played hard to get ... and she taunted him to distraction. Once she was sure she had him, she gave him what he wanted."

"Was she pregnant?" Maddie asked.

"Yes."

"When did you find out?"

"I knew before Jim did," Rose said. "The staff was loyal to me because they knew I would be loyal to them. When Jim tried to fire them for some imagined slight, I was the one who stepped in and smoothed things over.

"Rosario wasn't secretive about her desires," she said. "She told anyone who would listen that she was going to displace me from this house and claim Jim and his money for herself. I was rooting for her. I wanted Jim to divorce me."

"Why?"

"Because if I divorced him I would get nothing," Rose said. "If he divorced me I was due a payout. That's why I put up with him for as long as I did. I didn't want a lot, but I did want enough to buy a house. I figured we could share custody and everything would be okay."

"What happened?" Maddie asked.

"When Jim found out I wanted a payout to leave, he balked," Rose said. "He didn't want to give me money. For a rich man, he was pretty tight with the purse strings when he wanted to be. He and Rosario had plans to marry as soon as the ink was dry on our divorce. Jim put a stop to all of that when I refused to divorce him."

"How did Rosario take that?"

"Not well."

"Do you think ... is it possible ... ?"

"Are you asking me if Rosario killed me?"

"Yes."

"I can't be sure," Rose said. "She did wear a particular perfume, though, and that's the last thing I ever smelled."

Maddie felt inexplicably sad for the woman. "Why do you think you're still here, Rose?"

"At first I think I was hanging around until someone paid for killing me," Rose said. "I stopped caring about that years ago, though. Rosario never got what she wanted, so there was no reason to hold my anger close enough to darken my heart."

"So why are you still here now?"

"I don't think I can leave until ... he does."

Maddie stilled. "He who?"

"Jim," Rose said. "He's still here, too."

Things started to slip into place for Maddie. "Is he the poltergeist?"

"He's the anger," Rose said. "Look in there." She inclined her head toward a wooden door. "Be quick. I think he'll be here soon."

"Jim?"

"No," Rose said, shaking her head. "The other evil."

Maddie had no idea what that meant, but she was too keyed up to press Rose further. After fumbling with the loose handle for a few moments, Maddie pushed open the door and found herself staring into the bowels of ... Hell.

"Omigod."

24. TWENTY-FOUR

"Cassidy?"

The still form on the floor caused Maddie's heart to race. Cassidy's long, auburn hair was spread out around her face like a halo, and her usually peaches and cream complexion was waxy and ashen. Her hands were bound behind her back, and she was scrunched up into the fetal position. She was filthy, her top ripped at the shoulder, and her chest didn't appear to be moving.

"Cassidy?"

Maddie knelt down beside her. She was terrified to touch the woman, worried she would find death instead of life. She had no choice, though. When she pressed her fingers to Cassidy's neck, the woman jolted, causing Maddie to fall back on the ground.

"Holy crap," Maddie said, clutching at her heart. "You scared me."

Cassidy shifted her face to Maddie, taking a second to focus. "Maddie?"

"It's me," Maddie said, gasping. "Are you okay?"

"Is this a dream?" Cassidy's eyes were glassy and distant, and the red mark on her wrist tipped Maddie off that she'd been injected with something. "Do you know where you are?"

"I'm dead," Cassidy said, slurring her words slightly.

"You're not dead," Maddie said, crawling back toward the

confused woman. She tugged at the ropes holding her hands in place, but they wouldn't budge. "I'm going to find something to cut you loose. Hold on."

"I'm not going anywhere," Cassidy said. "You can't make me leave here. I'm dead."

"You're stoned is what you are," Maddie said, taking the opportunity to search the room. Rose was still standing in the doorway, her gaze fixed on Maddie. "Is there a knife around here or anything?"

Rose pointed toward a stack of boxes in the corner. Maddie scurried over and started searching through them, pausing as she realized there was more there than boxes. "What is all this?"

"The house has a past," Rose said.

"I get that," Maddie said. "Who is the woman in these photos?"

Rose floated over so she could see the photograph up close, frowning when the face swam into view. "That's Rosario."

"It is?"

Rose nodded.

"Why would these photos be down here?" Maddie asked.

"Maybe someone put them here after Rosario left."

"Are you sure Rosario left of her own accord?" Maddie asked.

"I have no idea where she went."

"That's not what I meant," Maddie said. "There's a rumor that Rosario never left. Some people say Big Jim killed her to keep the pregnancy a secret."

"Jim wouldn't do that," Rose said. "He didn't like to get his hands dirty."

"You said yourself that he didn't like to pay people, though," Maddie reminded her. "If Rosario was really pregnant, wouldn't he have killed her rather than pay for child support?"

"Perhaps," Rose said grudgingly. "I still don't think he would kill her. I think it's far more likely that he would pay to send her away. I didn't know a lot about Jim on a personal level, but I do know that prison wasn't something he would ever risk."

That made sense. Still, there was a piece of the puzzle Maddie was missing. "Who would've put all this stuff in here? Who knew about these passageways besides Jim?"

"Everyone knew," Rose said. "It's not like it was a secret."

Maddie rubbed her forehead, confused. "I just ... we're missing something."

"Who are you talking to?" Cassidy asked, staring at the ceiling. "Are you talking to a ghost?"

Maddie stilled. "What do you mean?"

"People in town say you can talk to ghosts," Cassidy said. "I thought they were blowing smoke up my ... huh, that's a weird saying. Who would blow smoke up there?"

"Hold on," Maddie said, returning to the boxes and rummaging about until she found an X-ACTO knife. She moved back to Cassidy and hunkered down beside her. "Hold still. I don't want to cut you."

"Why not? You've already ripped out my heart and stomped all over it," Cassidy said.

Maddie sighed, opting to remain quiet until she'd managed to saw through the cords binding Cassidy's wrists. The second her hands sprang free, Cassidy brought them around to her front with a groan.

"Oh, that hurts."

"Your circulation will come back in a few minutes," Maddie said. "It's going to be okay."

"Nothing is ever going to be okay again," Cassidy said. "It stopped being okay the second you came back to town and hypnotized Nick so you could steal him away from me."

"Is that what you really think happened?" Maddie asked.

"Yes."

Maddie opened her mouth to argue and then snapped it shut. There really was no reason to argue with the woman. She was confused and hurt. Now was not the time for this conversation. "How did you get here, Cassidy?"

"I was ... I was going to go to bed," Cassidy said, her mind traveling back to twenty-four hours before. "I was so tired. I was tired of it all. Marla made me go into those passageways upstairs. I didn't want to, but I did it anyway. I just didn't want to be alone.

"We were walking around, and Marla was complaining like she always does, and then we saw ... ."

"I know what you saw," Maddie said, fighting to rein in her temper. Given their current circumstances, getting in a fight about inappropriate spying seemed liked a bad idea. "Marla told us that you two were spying on us while we were ... going to bed."

"He never touched me that way," Cassidy said, her tone wistful. "He never kissed me that way. He never looked at me that way. I didn't want to see you two together, but I couldn't stop looking. It was like I was finally seeing what everyone – well, everyone except for Marla – had been telling me for months. Nick loves you."

"We love each other," Maddie said. "Marla said you two left the passageway and went back to your rooms. We found your necklace in front of the window. Did you go back?"

"I couldn't help myself," Cassidy said. "I was going to go to bed. I swear I was. I knew it was wrong to watch the two of you and yet ... I had to see. I had to be sure. I've been holding onto the idea of Nick begging me to give him another chance. I know it sounds pathetic, but there it is. I just needed to see you two together one more time. I needed you to shatter that illusion for me."

"I guess I get that," Maddie said. "It was still a violation. That was a private moment between him and me."

"I know," Cassidy said. "I just couldn't stop myself. When I got back, though, someone else was already there watching you."

"Who?"

"I thought it was Marla at first," Cassidy said. "The light wasn't very good in there. I had to drag her out the first time. She wanted to see Nick naked. It wasn't Marla, though."

"Who was it?"

"Me."

Maddie swiveled quickly, the sound of the new voice causing tremors to wrack her body. Instead of the amiable smile and ready grin she'd grown accustomed to over the past few days, though, Max's face was a mask of anger.

"Max."

"It seems we're finally going to get a chance to spend some time together after all, Maddie."

NICK WAS BEYOND FRUSTRATED. He'd found the passageway on the second floor without incident, but once inside he couldn't find a way to go anywhere else but the area he'd already explored. It was like the passageway existed in a world all its own.

He couldn't shake the feeling that Maddie was in trouble. Now that he'd landed on Max as a suspect, he knew he was on the right track. He still didn't know why Max would take Cassidy, though. He didn't even know if Cassidy was still alive. All he knew was that he had to find Maddie, and he had no idea where to look.

"I don't know if you can hear me, Olivia, but you have to help me," Nick said, hanging his head. "My Maddie needs me. I shouldn't have left her downstairs. I should have piled her in my truck this morning and taken her home. No, I should've never brought her here in the first place. I know this is all on me. I need you, though."

He waited for her to respond, but there was no answering whisper at the corners of his mind.

"She's in trouble, Olivia. I know it. She's in this house somewhere. You have to help me find her."

Nick was just about to give up when he ... felt ... something.

"This way," Olivia whispered.

"Where?" Nick asked. He couldn't see her, but her voice was strong and clear.

"Over here," Olivia said, her voice a little farther away.

Nick followed, confused, until he was in front of an old wardrobe. "Here?"

"Open it."

Nick did as instructed, and when he peered inside he almost wept with relief. Instead of old clothes, or even an empty box, he found a set of spiral stairs leading down into the guts of the house.

"Thank you," Nick said. "I promise I'll find her."

"Hurry," Olivia said. "She's not alone."

Nick didn't need to be told twice.

"WHAT'S GOING ON?" Maddie asked, leaving Cassidy on the floor and getting to her feet. She positioned herself between the vulnerable woman and Max as she considered what to do.

"Oh, don't do that, Maddie," Max said, his voice positively giddy. "You know very well what's going on here."

"No, I don't," Maddie said. "I just know I found Cassidy tied up in here. Did you do that?"

"Of course I did," Max said. "How else would I know where to look if I wasn't the one to bring her here?"

"I have no idea," Maddie said. "I do know that you probably could've gotten away with it if you didn't come down here now, though. Did you follow me?"

"I saw you leave the dining room," Max said. "I just had to know where you were going. I mean, you promised Nick you would stay in the dining room and then you immediately turned around and snuck out. What's that about?"

"I ... I had to go to the bathroom."

"In a secret passageway in the servants' quarters? That's an interesting lie."

"What makes you think I'm lying?" Maddie asked, shuffling back and forth. Max looked relatively normal, and yet there was something deranged about the way he was carrying himself. She had no way of knowing what was going on, and yet something told her she was about to solve more than one mystery.

"I heard you, Maddie," Max said, wagging his finger as if she was a naughty schoolgirl. "I was out in the hallway for quite some time before I came in. I heard you talking ... and it wasn't always to Cassidy. I'm dying to know who you were talking to."

"I was talking to myself."

"That's a lie," Max said. "Don't do that. I don't like it when people lie to me. I've had to live with it my whole life. I'm not going to put up with it now ... not when we're finally getting somewhere."

"I don't know what you mean," Maddie said, swallowing hard. "I was talking to myself. When I'm nervous, I do that."

"There have been rumors about you for a long time, Maddie," Max said, taking a step away from the door. "People say you can talk to ghosts. They say your mother could, too. Is that true?"

"That's ridiculous."

"I think you're just covering," Max said. "I'm not an idiot. You saw something in the mausoleum yesterday, didn't you? That's why Nick was so worked up. That's why you passed out. That's why you went back down there today."

"We were searching for Cassidy," Maddie said. "We were worried she locked herself in like I did."

"You're such a bad liar," Max said. "I don't understand why you're treating me like an idiot. I'm not one of those mindless morons downstairs. They might believe your falsehoods, but I don't. I know that you were talking to someone inside of the mausoleum. Nick was acting weird, and it was almost as if he was relieved when I finally left.

"I guess that means he knows that you talk to ghosts," Max mused. "Is that why you left after high school? Were you running away from what you can do? That's it, isn't it?"

"I don't know what you're talking about," Maddie said, risking a glance at Cassidy. For her part, the confused woman was still sitting on the floor and taking everything in. "Why did you grab Cassidy?"

"We're not done talking about you yet," Max said. "I want you to admit you were talking to a ghost at the mausoleum."

Maddie was caught. Max wasn't going to let it go. She didn't see where she had a lot of options. "Fine. I was talking to a ghost. Are you happy?"

"Who was it?"

"Rose Denton."

Max stilled, surprised. "Is that why you were asking so many questions about Big Jim down at dinner?"

"Yes. Rose was murdered. She was smothered in her bed. I was trying to figure out who did it."

"Isn't the obvious answer that it was Big Jim?"

"Except it was a woman who killed her," Maddie said, seeing no reason to lie. "Rose could smell her perfume while it was happening."

"What woman?" Max asked, intrigued.

"It was a former maid here," Maddie said. "Her name was Rosario Torres."

While his face was relaxed before, almost as if he was toying with her, Max's features took on an ugly quality after Maddie's admission. "That's a lie."

Maddie had no idea why he was so upset. "No, it's not," Maddie said. "Rosario Torres seduced Jim Denton because she wanted to be the lady of the house. When Rose refused to divorce him without a payout, Jim decided he wasn't going to divorce her. Rosario had no choice but to kill Rose."

"Stop saying that!"

"Why? It's the truth. It's not like it affects you."

"That's where you're wrong," Max said. "It affects me very much. You see, I'm not just Aaron Denton's best friend. I'm his cousin. You're not maligning some random maid. You're making up stories about my grandmother. I'm not going to stand for that."

Maddie shifted her eyes to Rose, things finally slipping into place.

"He has her eyes," Rose said. "I should've seen it a long time ago."

Maddie knew she was in serious trouble now, and she had no idea how to get out of it.

"Rosario Torres is your grandmother?"

"She was," Max said. "She died when I was six."

Maddie rolled the idea through her mind, finally deciding that it actually made sense. Well, it would, as soon as she clarified a few details. "That means your mother was Big Jim's daughter, doesn't it?"

"Very good," Max said, taking another step into the room and closing the distance between them. "How much of this have you figured out?"

"I know that Rosario came to this house with the express intention to seduce Big Jim," Maddie said. "She wanted to get pregnant. She thought if she could make sure he was infatuated with her that she would be able to control him."

"Big Jim seduced my grandmother," Max countered. "She was innocent until he put his filthy hands on her."

"That's a lie," Rose said. "Rosario was never innocent."

Maddie ignored her. "When your grandmother found out she was pregnant, she pressured Big Jim about marrying her. He wouldn't divorce Rose, though. She wanted money to leave and he didn't want to give her any."

"My grandmother always said that woman was a bitter shrew,"

Max said. "She just didn't want Big Jim and my grandmother to be happy. That was her way of punishing them."

"I don't understand why Big Jim and your grandmother didn't get married after Rose died," Maddie said. "Granny told me that everyone in town expected Jim to put on a big show and mourn Rose for a few months before marrying Rosario."

"That was the plan," Max said. "Big Jim promised my grandmother the world. He told her she wouldn't have to wait forever. It was just supposed to be a few months. She was going to get everything she ever wanted."

"What happened?"

"Because of her fragile condition, my grandmother wasn't capable of keeping a house this size up," Max said. "She was put on bed rest in her sixth month. Big Jim hired a new maid to take over her duties."

"I'm guessing those duties were the same ones your grandmother had been performing for him," Maddie said. "He cheated on her, didn't he?"

"He wasn't even sorry he did it," Max said, his face twisting. "He told my grandmother that he was going to give her the world and then he yanked the rug right out from under her. She confronted him about all of it. She told him that cheating wasn't going to be allowed when they got married. Do you know what he told her?"

Maddie had a feeling she did. "He told her he had no intention of marrying her," Maddie said, glancing at Rose for support. The ghost merely nodded, encouraging her to continue. "I think Big Jim realized that he was finally free of his wife, and despite how attracted he was to your grandmother, he decided he wanted to plow a few other fields instead of settling down."

"That's a pretty good guess," Max said. "Can you believe he did that? He just threw my grandmother away like she was garbage. He even told her she couldn't have her job back after she gave birth to the baby."

"Did he ever pay child support?"

"Of course not," Max said. "You have to remember, this was the 1960s. It wasn't so easy to demand a paternity test. They existed back then, but they were very costly. Big Jim essentially tossed my grandmother out of this house and never looked back. He didn't even care about the baby. That was his daughter, and he didn't care."

"What happened to your grandmother?"

"She moved to Traverse City and found a job as a secretary after she gave birth," Max said. "She raised my mother all on her own, and eventually she got married and had another child. She never got over what Big Jim did to her, though. It marked her."

"Did your mother know who her father was?"

"She found some paperwork in my grandmother's things when she was cleaning one day," Max said. "She couldn't believe what she found. I was only three at the time, and she didn't tell me any of it until I was much older."

"She knew who Big Jim was when she took the job as a maid, though, didn't she?"

"Of course she did," Max said. "She went to college to be a para-legal, and yet she ended up working as a maid. Do you know why that is?"

"She wanted to get to know her father," Maddie supplied. "She thought that was the best way."

"You're a smart little cookie," Max said, winking. "It's the rare woman who has beauty and brains. I'm looking forward to exploring your beauty when we're done here."

He was going to be waiting a long time for that. Maddie was just stalling now. She knew Nick would be looking for her. She had faith he would find her. Just like in the mausoleum, Nick would find a way to get to her – even if he had to rely on a little help from a ghostly friend.

"Did your mother tell Big Jim who she was?" Maddie asked.

"She was going to," Max said. "Then he tried to grope her in the hallway one day. She was ... disgusted. Her own father was trying to touch her."

"I don't want to make excuses for Big Jim, but there was no way he could know who your mother was if she didn't tell him," Maddie said.

"He should've known the second he saw her," Max seethed. "She was his blood. You're supposed to recognize your blood."

"You lived in this house for years," Maddie said, her mind turning as she tried to put the final pieces of the puzzle together. "Your mother made a decision to keep her secret at some point. She decided to stay the course. When did you find out the truth?"

"I stumbled across it by accident really," Max said. "I was fifteen years old. I found these photos." He gestured toward the box in the corner. "It took me a little while to figure out what was going on, but when I confronted my mother, she admitted the truth.

"Do you have any idea what that was like? I lived like a second-class citizen in this house for years," he said. "I was nothing more than the maid's son. Aaron tried to be nice to me, but I could always see that he was looking down on me. There was no one else for him to play with, so he decided I could be his pity friend."

"Aaron loves you," Maddie said. "He doesn't look down on you. You may have convinced yourself of that, but it's not true. That's not who Aaron is."

"You don't even know him," Max said. "He puts on a show for people ... just like his mother. He's a snob."

"What did you do when you found out the truth?" Maddie asked. She already knew the answer. She'd finally figured it all out. She needed Max to confirm it.

"What do you think I did? I confronted Big Jim."

"What did he do?"

"He laughed at me," Max said. "There I was, a fifteen-year-old kid who thought he was about to be embraced by his grandfather, and he laughed at me. He told me my grandmother was a whore and there was no way I was ever going to see a dime from him because he didn't believe I was his grandson.

"He told me that he didn't care about my mother, and if he had the chance he would still have sex with her," he continued, raw emotion pouring out of him now. "He called her filthy names, and he commented on her body. It was disgusting. He knew what he was doing. He was just trying to get a rise out of me."

"He was an awful man," Rose said. "Oh, he was so much worse than I realized."

"You killed him, didn't you?" Maddie asked, gazing at Max expectantly.

"How could you possibly know that?"

"Because only someone killed in a fit of rage could carry that much rage over to the other side," Maddie said, realizing why Big Jim turned into a poltergeist rather than moving on. "Aaron said his grandfather died when he was fifteen. He didn't say how he died. How did you get away with killing him?"

"He was walking away from me," Max said. "His back was to me. I was blind with anger. I couldn't help myself. He was halfway up the stairs when I caught up with him. I grabbed his shoulder. I wanted him to take it all back. He wouldn't, though, so I just ... threw him down the stairs.

"He kind of bounced his way down," Max said. "I could tell his neck was broken by the way he landed. I was going to run down to him. I was going to try and help him, I swear I was, but then I heard someone coming from the main hallway and I did the only thing I could do."

"You ran and never said a thing about it," Maddie said.

"I made a choice that day," Max said. "Jim Denton refused to acknowledge me, so I refused to acknowledge what I did."

"Your mother quit her job not long after the death, didn't she? I seem to remember you moving to town when you were about that age. Did you tell her what you did?"

"No," Max said. "I never told anyone ... until now. She had her suspicions, though. That's why she insisted on getting me out of this house. She never understood, though. This house should've been mine. I should've grown up here. I should've had my own room on the second floor. I shouldn't have been hidden in the basement like some dirty little secret."

"What happened to your family wasn't right," Maddie said. "Jim Denton was a particular kind of animal. That doesn't mean what you've done is okay. You killed him. You kidnapped Cassidy. Why did you do that, by the way?"

"I couldn't have her telling Nick that I was watching the two of you," Max said. "You see, the thing is, I didn't just come back to this house to see Aaron. I didn't come back because of the memories. I came back because of you, too."

Maddie's heart lodged in her throat. "What do you mean?"

"When Aaron told me you were back in town I realized I had a shot at claiming more than my birthright," Max said. "I knew I had a shot at making you mine, too. I always wanted you. I always knew we were supposed to be together. Nick was the one standing in our way. He ruined our chance back then, but he's not going to ruin it now. We're going to have a good life together, Maddie. We're going to make this house our own."

"You've lost your mind," Maddie said. "If you think for a second that I would ever touch you, you're crazy."

"I just told you that I'm entitled to half of this fortune," Max snapped. "I'm going to be a rich man. Don't you want to live this life with me?"

"I already have a life," Maddie said. "It's with Nick. It's never going to be with you."

"You say that now," Max said. "Once I take care of the Nick problem, though, you're going to change your mind. I can guarantee it."

"How are you going to take care of Nick?"

"It's easy," Max said. "I'm going to kill him. I'm going to kill Cassidy, too. Once they both disappear, people will think they took off together. It's perfect. You'll be left behind, and you'll have to pretend you're broken-hearted for a few weeks, but after that people will be thrilled that we found each other."

He was delusional. There was no way around it. He honestly believed she was going to fall in love with him after he admitted he was a murderer. "I'm never going to be with you, Max."

"Never say never. There's nothing standing in our way now, Maddie. We can have everything."

"There's one thing standing in your way."

Maddie had no idea how long Nick had been standing there, but the look on his face told her he'd heard at least a portion of Max's story. Max jumped when he saw him, fear flitting across his features as he realized his happily ever after was about to take a turn. "How did you find us?"

"I had a little help," Nick said, his gaze touching on Maddie before returning to the threat in the room. "How do you think you're going to get away with this, Max?"

"I've got it all planned out," Max said. "I'm going to kill you and Cassidy and bury your bodies in the woods. I had to keep Cassidy alive long enough to kill you together, just in case your bodies were discovered. Once that's taken care of, I'm going to tell Aaron the truth and if he refuses to give me what's mine then I'm going to sue him and take it."

"You can't sue Aaron because your grandfather refused to acknowledge you," Nick said, forcing himself to remain calm. "Big Jim had an ironclad will. A judge isn't going to overturn that."

"I have biology on my side."

"It doesn't matter," Nick said. "People leave blood relatives out of their wills all the time. It doesn't mean a thing. You're not going to get a piece of the Denton pie. You're not a Denton. You never were."

"You don't know what you're talking about," Max said, his mind clearly working overtime. "I ... no ... I have this all planned out."

"Well, you're done," Nick said. "You're not going to hurt Cassidy, and I can guarantee you're never going to lay a hand on Maddie. I'll kill you first."

"You're going to have to," Max said. "This is the life I've been dreaming of for as long as I can remember. No one is keeping me from it." Max moved quickly, launching himself at Nick. Nick must have been expecting it, though, because he caught him in midair and slammed him into the wall behind him.

Maddie glanced over at Cassidy, finding the woman much more alert than she had been a few minutes before. "Get up," she instructed. "Move over by that wall."

Cassidy didn't argue. Maddie followed her away from the fight, knowing she couldn't help Nick. She was a distraction, and she wasn't going to put him at risk. Rose was still hovering in the corner, her face a mask of horror and sadness as she watched the two men grapple with each other. She seemed lost in thought until a high-pitched keening shattered the tableau.

"He's coming," Rose said, turning to Maddie with a fearful expression on her face. "It's Jim. He's here."

"He's coming for Max," Maddie said. "Max killed him and then left. When that happened, all the rage Big Jim was feeling at the moment of his death had nowhere to go. Once Max returned, Big Jim had an outlet."

"Are you sure?" Rose asked.

"I'm sure," Maddie said, turning her attention back to the fight and moving toward Nick with a purpose. She had to separate the two men, and she had to do it now.

Nick slammed Max's head into the hard floor, jolting him twice and knocking him senseless. He was about to do it a third time when Maddie stilled him with a hand on his shoulder. "That's enough," she said.

"Do you have any idea what he was going to do to you, Maddie?"

"I do," Maddie said. "Come with me."

"What?" Nick was incredulous.

The wailing increased to a point where Maddie wasn't the only one who could hear it.

"What is that?" Cassidy asked, clamping her hands over her ears.

"Retribution," Maddie said, tugging on Nick's arm and pulling him away from Max.

"Maddie, what are you doing?"

At that moment, a bright light exploded in the center of the room. Big Jim's poltergeist was screaming as his ethereal hands reached for Max. In his final moments, recognition washed over Max's face. He saw his own killer, just like Big Jim did the night he died. Nick instinctively sheltered Maddie with his body, covering her head as Max began to scream.

Max didn't stop screaming until the final breath left his body.

26. TWENTY-SIX

"Does someone want to tell me what happened here?"

Dawn climbed the horizon a few hours after emergency personnel arrived. Dale Kreskin wasn't far behind, and after collecting evidence and checking the body, he was now delving into the big questions. The inhabitants of the Denton mansion were exhausted, but they had answers to give – even if some people were reticent to supply them.

Aaron was in shock as Max's body was hauled out of the basement. Nick pulled him aside long enough to explain everything. Disbelief and grief crippled Aaron quickly, and now he was sitting on the ground and staring at the rising sun. There was nothing anyone could do for him – not now, at least – so they left him with his thoughts and regret. He'd lost his best friend and cousin in one fell swoop. This wasn't something he was ever going to be able to wrap his mind around without time to digest it.

Nick rocked Maddie in his arms as Kreskin questioned them. He needed her close. He had no idea how he was going to explain the poltergeist, especially since it dissipated in the immediate aftermath of Max's death. Surprisingly, Cassidy handled it for him.

"He was crazy," she said. "Nick saved us. I think he must have hit his head when he fell."

"Is that what happened?" Kreskin asked, clearly suspicious.

"Yes," Nick said, shooting Cassidy a grateful look.

"Well, I guess that's as good of an explanation as any," Kreskin said. "Cassidy, you should probably go to the hospital. We have no idea what Max shot you up with."

"Sure," Cassidy said, pulling the blanket the paramedics supplied her with tighter around her neck. "I just want to talk to Nick and Maddie for a minute first."

Kreskin merely nodded and moved down the lawn in Aaron's direction. Nick knew he didn't believe their story. Most of it was true, but Max's death was hard to explain. Kreskin couldn't argue with three witnesses, though, and it didn't appear that he wanted to.

"Thank you for finding me, Maddie," Cassidy said sincerely. "I would've died down there if it wasn't for you."

"I didn't do anything that anyone else wouldn't have done," Maddie said.

"Yes, you did," Cassidy said. "I ... I'm not sure that we can ever be friends. There's always going to be a part of me that believes you took something from me."

Ironically, Maddie knew exactly how she felt.

"I am sorry for spying on you, though, and I promise I won't make more problems for the two of you," Cassidy said. "I know now that you two love each other. I know you were destined to be together. It still hurts, but it's time I get over it. You're happy, and I need to find a way to be happy myself.

"I don't know how I'm going to do it," she continued. "I do know that I'm going to do it, though. I want what you have. I just need to find someone who wants it with me."

"You'll find it," Nick said, rubbing soothing circles on Maddie's back as he kept her tight against his chest. "You're a good person. I have faith you'll find everything you want in life."

"I hope so," Cassidy said. "The good news for me is that the paramedic is kind of hot."

Maddie smiled. She couldn't help herself. "Good luck."

"You, too."

Once it was just the two of them, Nick turned his somber brown eyes to Maddie. "You're in trouble, love."

"What?"

"You promised me you were going to stay in the dining room," Nick said. "You broke that promise."

"Rose showed up. I had to follow her."

"Speaking of Rose, where is she?"

"Big Jim's poltergeist was the one keeping her here," Maddie said. "At first it was her anger. She let that go a long time ago, though. She should've been able to cross over then. He trapped her here. He needed someone to control, and she was his only option. As soon as he left, she was able to go."

"Are you sure he left?"

"I felt him leave," Maddie said. "He was trapped here until he could express his rage. The only one he could do that with was Max. Ironically, if Max had stayed away longer, Big Jim would still be haunting his precious house."

"So both Big Jim and Rose are gone?"

"Yes."

"You're still in trouble," Nick said.

"Nicky, I didn't mean to break my promise," Maddie said, earnestness washing over her face. "I had to follow Rose. I had to find Cassidy. If I hadn't done it ... ."

"Cassidy would probably be dead," Nick finished.

"And you, too."

"I was already suspicious of Max," Nick said. "There's no way he could've gotten the drop on me."

"We'll just have to agree to disagree," Maddie said. "I really am sorry. I would never purposely lie to you."

Nick sighed, weariness getting the better of him. He lowered his mouth and kissed her softly. "I'm going to let it go, love. I'm too tired to fight."

"What happens now?"

"Now Kreskin has his suspicions, but he won't be able to prove anything," Nick said. "We're going to go upstairs and spend exactly five minutes packing up our stuff. Then we're going to drive to our home and go to bed for the rest of the day."

"Our home?"

"Our home," Nick confirmed. "We're never going to be apart again, Mad. That's a promise I'm going to make to you, and I'll never break it."

"I promise that I'll always love you," Maddie said.

"Good," Nick said. "I can't imagine living the rest of this life – or the next – without you."

"You'll never have to."

Nick kissed Maddie one more time and then started pulling her toward the house. He was eager to collect their belongings and leave the Denton mansion. What started as a reunion had ended in tragedy. They still had a happy home of their own to enjoy, though.

"Nicky?"

"Hmm."

"I don't suppose you'd be willing to stop at the diner for breakfast on our way home, would you? I'm starving."

Nick considered the suggestion. "We'll get it to go," he said. "I wasn't joking when I said we were spending the day in bed."

"I promise to enjoy every second of it," Maddie teased.

That was a promise they were both eager to keep.

Made in the USA
Monee, IL
12 June 2022

97898546R00121